BLURRED LINES

BLURRED LINES

AUDREY NOTTINGHAM

ARCHWAY
PUBLISHING

This is a work of fiction. All of the characters, names, incidents,
organizations, and dialogue in this novel are either the products
of the author's imagination or are used fictitiously.

Archway Publishing books may be ordered through booksellers or by contacting:

Archway Publishing
1663 Liberty Drive
Bloomington, IN 47403
www.archwaypublishing.com
844-669-3957

Because of the dynamic nature of the Internet, any web addresses or
links contained in this book may have changed since publication and
may no longer be valid. The views expressed in this work are solely those
of the author and do not necessarily reflect the views of the publisher,
and the publisher hereby disclaims any responsibility for them.

Any people depicted in stock imagery provided by Getty Images are
models, and such images are being used for illustrative purposes only.
Certain stock imagery © Getty Images.

ISBN: 978-1-6657-4084-5 (sc)
ISBN: 978-1-6657-4085-2 (hc)
ISBN: 978-1-6657-4086-9 (e)

Library of Congress Control Number: 2023905207

Print information available on the last page.

Archway Publishing rev. date: 4/25/2023

CHAPTER
ONE

Kat spotted him sitting cross-legged at a café they used to frequent for brunch. He was with *her*. Kat's nemesis. The woman sleeping with her husband. She was lovely. She was all the things Kat no longer was, including his confidante, the outlet he sought. Kat had lost her control over him. She was no longer his desire, only an obligation. Kat lived in his house, made sure his clothes were taken to and picked up from the dry cleaner's, and sat at his dinner table. As she watched from across the street, her fists balled up tightly, and her heart beat like a drum against her chest. She felt as if she had been left behind.

Kat and her husband, Ryan, hadn't been to that café in two years. She remembered their last time there, when she'd announced she was pregnant. He'd been delighted; his smile had been genuine. That day was marked in her mind forever; they had been happy then. It had been a beautiful moment, and she often thought about that day. The sun had gleamed, and the sky had been the perfect shade of blue. After the café, they had visited Central Park and laid a blanket down to watch the world around them persevere. The passersby had seemed preoccupied, though Kat and Ryan had not been. They had been lost in love, in lust, and in the future. They had been passionately enthralled in each other then.

⟐

As Kat finished preparing dinner, she heard the front door open. The recollection of Ryan and Sophia having lunch together earlier that day was on her mind as Ryan suddenly emerged in the kitchen.

"How was work?" she asked him as he loosened his tie.

The tie was navy silk. She had given it to him the day before he'd been promoted five years ago. She'd told him it would bring him good luck.

"The same as every other day," he replied as he made his way out of the kitchen and to their bedroom hurriedly.

He was distant, which was nothing new; he had been distant for months. They rarely diverted from routine conversation these days.

Ryan was a good-looking, smart, ambitious man, a go-getter type—a keeper, her friend Amy had told her after introducing them six years ago. He was tall and blond, with green eyes. He looked as if he had spent every summer on a surfboard in California, chiseled abs and all, and he was now the CFO of one of the largest pharmaceutical companies in New York. She'd won the lottery when she met him; he was going places, and she knew it.

Amy had been dating Tom, who'd had a single friend, Ryan, from the gym. Amy always described Kat as shy and mysterious. She was usually the last one to speak up and rarely called attention to herself. Amy had to ask Kat what was on her mind, as she never naturally volunteered information. Back then, Ryan had seemed intrigued by Kat, as if he'd yearned to know her. He had lingered on every word she spoke, waiting for her next sentence.

Kat had begun her career working for a small-scale newspaper in Manhattan as an editor, way beneath her potential. She seldom did the party scene. Her friends called her lame. She was OK with it. She spent most evenings in with a bottle of chardonnay and a book.

One evening, Amy had refused to take no for an answer. Kat had been bullied, and she'd caved. That night, she'd been pleased she had after spotting Ryan, her unsuspecting blind date. Kat's first impression had been that he was charming, outgoing, and confident. He had to be, she'd assumed, to climb the ladder of success so quickly. The ladies had ogled at him from across the room, but Ryan never had seemed to notice. His words had been clever, and he'd made direct eye contact, sometimes holding it for so long that Kat finally had to look away. His body language had been relaxed, as if he owned the room. Never once had he looked over his shoulder or appeared insecure.

Eventually, Ryan had begun leaving her rousing love notes and calling her throughout the day just to ask her how her day was going. He even had whisked her away on little getaways here and there after they became serious.

As they sat for dinner, Kat reflected on how things had changed from past to present. Awkward silence now filled the room. Kat had purposely prepared his favorite meal: sukiyaki, a Japanese dish that required effort, and German chocolate cake, his favorite dessert. Kat knew he had just sat with the other woman earlier that day, and it made Kat's blood boil. One could have cut the tension with a knife. She wanted him to feel something for her. She wanted him to feel guilt more than anything. If he did feel guilty, he hid it well. She saw no signs of remorse or shame.

He ate every bite of his meal and walked to the kitchen.

She followed. "I missed you today."

He didn't reply for a moment. He placed his dish in the sink and gulped down his last swallow of wine. "I'm sorry I wasn't able to make it home for lunch today. My meeting ran long," he finally replied.

The lie poured out of his mouth easily, with no second thought at all. He hadn't even bothered to call.

"Did you close the deal?" she asked. He had been working to win over a potential client for weeks.

"There are still some details to work out, but it looks promising."

More work banter followed. Sadly, that was what the relationship had devolved into. She was torn. She felt rage and sadness at the same time. Was she to blame for the downfall of their marriage? Even so, how was he able to look her in the eye and lie without hesitation? This was now normal. She had become obsessed with his days and not her own. She hadn't worked since she lost the baby. She had lost her baby, her job, and her husband. She followed him most days. She had become infatuated with his every step—and the other woman.

The other woman was Sophia Gantz, an attorney at Hall and Associates, one of the largest law firms in Manhattan. She had made partner about two years ago and moved into a swanky apartment in NoHo. Not only was she successful, but she was also gorgeous, well traveled, and cultured. She and Ryan had plenty in common. On paper, they were a better match. Sophia was tall and thin, with long black hair. Her eyes were so blue that one could almost see through them. Her eyes reminded

Kat of the ocean. It was the prettiest color of blue Kat had ever seen—piercing. Her perfect jawline and stunning lips captivated Kat. Kat knew exactly why Ryan was drawn to Sophia. She had never been married and, until Ryan, had never even been involved in a serious relationship that Kat could verify, although according to her social media, she had plenty of gentlemen acquaintances. She'd graduated from Boston University, ranking fourth in her class. She appeared motivated and impressive, according to Kat's research. She had soared up the ladder of achievement and not with her looks, although Kat was sure they had helped. Kat had the impression that Sophia was spectacular and glamourous, and it intimated Kat. Even on her morning runs, Sophia looked as if she had first dominated the runway. Kat often wondered if that was how she woke up. *Could she naturally be this breathtaking?*

Kat had begun following Sophia regularly after she discovered Sophia was Ryan's mistress. Kat had suspected Ryan was being untruthful regarding his whereabouts after several late nights and no offer of any explanations, so she'd decided to tail him. That had been when she discovered his extramarital activities and Sophia. She then had become entwined in Sophia's routine. Her favorite coffee shop, the store where she purchased her groceries—her schedule was etched into Kat's brain. Curiosity had driven her at first, and then it had become her obsession, like oxygen to her, an uncontrollable fixation. Kat had a void to fill after Noah.

CHAPTER
TWO

Noah had been stillborn. The nursery was still just as it had been. The door remained closed, but Kat often went in and gazed at the pale blue walls. The gray rocking chair was comforting to her. She would sit there for hours and shed tears. It wasn't healthy. Kat knew that, but it made her feel close to Noah—close to what could have been.

After the funeral, Kat rarely emerged from bed. For weeks, she buried herself in grief, unbothered by the life that remained outside her bedroom. Kat recognized that Ryan attempted to comfort her, but she realized he was struggling to tend to his own sorrow as well. She knew he was grieving, but he always remained silent, seeming to choose her grief over his own. Ryan appeared at times as lost as she was. When she would look him in the eye, his eyes were empty. He stopped smiling and wore a frown most days, just going through the motions of staying alive. Kat never truly acknowledged aloud the pain Ryan experienced as she abandoned him and herself. Kat left him alone and vulnerable.

After she lost Noah, Kat eventually lost her job at the paper too. She was let go. She had missed a considerable amount of work, and the company had to replace her. Ryan went back to work almost immediately after Noah passed; he had responsibilities to manage. He would call frequently to check in on Kat, always receiving the same answer: "I'm fine." Everyone knew she wasn't fine. Most of her friends had stopped calling. Amy would stop in about once a week to make sure she was breathing and occasionally lie in bed with Kat for hours, rarely conversing. Amy would have dinner at the house with Ryan, and sometimes Tom would join. They occasionally went out for dinner as well, leaving Kat at home solo. For months, this continued.

Ryan eventually talked Kat into therapy. Once a week, she would travel downtown to sit in an office with a tan couch and a therapist named Sheila. She usually focused on the round clock beside the bookcase and counted down the hour. It didn't help. She never felt closure. Sheila wasn't able to fix her. She wasn't able to tell Kat why this had happened and when this feeling of emptiness would subside. It was useless, in Kat's mind. She would lie to Ryan about the progress she made, but she assumed he knew better. However, she was leaving the house clothed and with teeth brushed, which Kat decided was progress. She went for a month.

Kat noticed Ryan threw himself into work, and she didn't blame him, with all the loneliness she held on to. She had changed. She was no longer his lover; she was a lost soul living in the palace he had bought for her and Noah. She was certain the place no longer felt like home to Ryan; it was just where he sat for dinner, showered, and slept. He always managed to make it home for dinner to check on Kat, but it was not unusual for him to return to his office after eating. He felt obligated, and Kat sensed it. Still, Kat was relieved that Ryan had not abandoned her; she could see the glimmer of hope he was holding on to that Kat would defeat the black hole she was hiding in.

Eventually, the spark faded, and she could no longer see it, when she cared to look for it.

❦

Ryan met Sophia a few months after Noah died. She was representing a client he was pursuing. She was charming. Her laugh was addicting. He couldn't remember the last time he had heard Kat laugh. He knew his thoughts were inappropriate as he watched her across the table during business meetings, wondering what her skin felt like. It appeared soft and slightly sun-kissed, like a dream. She smelled like a hint of pine trees, clean and fresh. It reminded him of a hiking trip in Oregon he had once taken with Kat. Sophia was sociable, funny, and clever—just what he needed that evening. Reaching an agreement that night meant he would see her again. He had never been more excited about work.

Ryan was a good man. Or he used to be. He was a good husband, until he wasn't. He didn't have the courage to leave Kat, and he wasn't even sure he wanted to. Ryan had grown up with a single mother who worked hard to provide for him. She was encouraging and supportive; she told Ryan he was capable of anything, and he believed her. She loved him dearly. Kat reminded Ryan of his mother. Eve cherished Kat and knew how much Kat loved her son. She told Ryan she could tell it in the way Kat looked at him. He respected his mother more than anyone. Before she passed, she and Ryan had a long conversation about marriage and love, and Eve revealed that Ryan's father had deserted her while she was pregnant with

Ryan. He never had known that. He never had asked. All he'd known was Eve. It had always been the two of them.

Eve said she was desperately in love with his father, a free-spirited artist who wasn't ready to be a father or settle down. After Ryan's dad left, Eve got a job as a secretary for some bigwig information security analyst in Manhattan. Eve was pretty—so beautiful that she was given the job over someone more qualified, because the higher-ups believed the office needed a facelift to appear attractive. Eve was smart; she was good at her job. She made decent money and was able to financially support Ryan on her own.

She told Ryan she thought about his dad every day, and she believed in true love even still. She told him she knew Kat was his love story. He held on to his mother's words. Kat was by Eve's side until she passed, mostly chatting about Noah and what he would become. Kat's job was much more flexible than Ryan's, so she was able to be there. She would visit Eve daily to give her meds and help her shower. Ryan paid someone to be in the home with Eve, but Kat went anyway. Ryan would go when he could, but he had just been promoted and had heavy obligations at work. Kat felt it was her duty to be with Eve, but the truth was, she loved Eve. She had grown close to Eve.

Kat had been raised by her grandparents after her parents died in a car crash when she was two years old. Her sister, Maggie, who had been five at the time, also had died in the wreck. Kat couldn't remember Maggie or her parents. She only knew them from photos her grandparents had had on display throughout their home. Her grandparents had passed within the same year Kat turned nineteen. She had been on her own after that. Eve filled a void left by something that had been missing for a long time. Eve was motherly, and she immediately took to Kat and treated her as her own.

Ryan knew the bond between his mother and Kat was strong. Whenever he considered leaving Kat, the guilt would become overwhelming. He didn't want to disappoint his mother or break his promise he'd made to always take care of Kat. Meeting Sophia was unexpected. The feelings were unexpected.

CHAPTER
THREE

Ryan winked at Kat from across the table. It was Kat's first blind date. She certainly did not plan on taking a complete stranger home with her that evening. Yet Ryan didn't feel like a stranger to her. She fell in love with him that very night. He ignited an intensity in her she was unfamiliar with. She was completely at his mercy from the start. He eventually made his way around the table.

He cocked one eyebrow as he spoke. "What are your intentions with me tonight, Katherine Benson?" He was handsome, and he knew it. He looked her straight in the eye as he waited for her to answer. He was wearing a Columbia University T-shirt, with his hair parted to the side and a surfer's tan. He looked as if he had grown up in California, not New York. Amy had given her a quick rundown on him before forcing her to go out that evening, so Kat knew a little bit about him beforehand.

"I'm assuming that line typically works for you?" she snidely replied as she clutched her glass and took a sip. She could flirt. She was shy, but she was capable. There was something about him that made her defenseless and weak for him.

"It's loud in here; I can't hear you. We should get out of

here. Maybe take a walk," he said, although he appeared to have heard her loud and clear. He came across as witty and overly self-assured. Kat recognized this was an attempt to get her alone.

Amy and Tom were taking shots and laughing, unaware of Ryan and Kat's attendance. Amy was the fun girl, always overindulged and entertained, the life of the party. Kat and Amy had been roommates in college by chance and happened to be complete opposites. They'd decided they balanced each other out pretty well.

Kat yelled at Amy across the table, "I need to go to the bathroom! Come with me."

Ryan still stood beside Kat's stool. Amy obliged and left her barstool after dramatically planting one on Tom. Kat batted her eyes and walked away, saying nothing to Ryan. Amy followed Kat to the restroom.

"Are you sure he's not a serial killer or—I don't know—a weirdo?" Kat asked Amy.

"You want to find out, don't you, Kat?" Amy said as she nudged Kat against the sink with her elbow and giggled. "Jesus Christ, Kat, no, I told you. He's a good guy—a keeper, from what I hear. Tom works out with him pretty much daily, and I'm guessing he would have mentioned that. Get yourself laid. Or who knows? Married." She rolled her eyes and walked out, leaving Kat alone in the bathroom. Amy always insisted Kat was an overthinker and always stressed, accusing her of never being in the moment.

Kat returned to the table; Amy was leaning on Tom, with Ryan on the other side.

"Another round of shots!" Amy yelled as she held her glass up for the bartender.

Ryan said, "Count Katherine and me out; we are taking a

walk. She insists. I'm sorry, you two." He looked at Amy and Tom. "She plans to make me hers." He then turned to Kat and grabbed her hand.

Kat threaded her fingers in between his and followed him out willingly through the cloud of smoke and bargoers.

Kat turned her head toward Amy as she was leaving, and Amy sliced her neck with an invisible knife and started laughing. Kat flipped her off as they exited the bar.

"Call me Kat," she told Ryan as they walked. The night was perfect, warm with a breeze. Crowded streets were humming and bustling, although she didn't notice. Chills penetrated Kat's body, making her tremble. She released her hand from his, still trying to figure out what in the hell she was thinking. *Leaving with a stranger Amy insists is a great guy. Yeah, cool, Kat. Sounds like a good plan.* She scolded herself. The connection, though, gave Kat shivers and made her heart pound.

"OK, Kat. Well, you're welcome," he replied.

"Oh yeah? I'm welcome? For what, may I ask?" she said.

"For my rescuing you from a morning of dry heaves and a punishing headache." He laughed.

"Fine, thank you. Although clearly, you haven't heard I'm the responsible friend." She smirked.

Ryan responded, "I have heard a little, but I'd love to hear more."

They walked for three hours that night, chatting and flirting, bouncing off each other naturally. Kat had been in relationships previously, but none had been serious. She had never been awestruck with someone. He was also the opposite of Kat: adventurous. He had dreams of travel and adventure, making those things appear tempting to Kat.

They eventually made their way to her apartment. Ryan stood in front of her, looking up at her building.

"I don't want this night to end," he blurted out.

Relief washed over her. She felt the same. She calmed her nerves and gripped his hand softly, gently pulling him toward the door with her.

That night, Kat surrendered herself to Ryan. She didn't think twice about losing her self-control and served herself on a silver platter. She felt no shame. Loaded with security, she made him hers that night. That was the beginning.

Kat and Ryan never spent another night apart. Ryan was thriving at work, and Kat supported him every step of the way. They were more than lovers; they were best friends. Just like Kat and Amy, she and Ryan had a balance. He coaxed her into risky adventures or trips she never would have typically agreed on, such as sneaking into concerts, staying out late and carousing, and escaping to Mexico spontaneously without an inkling of a plan. On the other hand, she kept him grounded with cozy nights in front of the fire and focusing on his health. She always made sure he did his yearly physical and other things he found irrelevant or placed on the back burner. Each appreciated the other. With the stability and the compromise, it worked.

Kat wanted to be a mother. Ryan wanted to be a father. There was nothing they had not discussed after four years dating. A week after their four-year anniversary, it became clear to Kat that Ryan was ready to take the next step.

"Hey, baby, how was your day?" Kat asked as Ryan walked through the door. He walked toward her and slapped her ass as he set his briefcase down on the floor.

"This apartment is too small, Kat," he answered.

She looked at him, confused. "I love our apartment," she said as she bounced her head back.

The apartment was a tiny one-bedroom near Ryan's office and not too far from Kat's. It was perfect for them. It was on the third floor and had a doorman. They had picked it out together, deciding they needed nothing more.

"It's too small. Where are we going to put the nursery?" he asked as he picked her up with both hands, squeezing her body close to his.

Kat was on board with expanding their family, so they began trying. Five months later, Kat was pregnant with Noah.

After Noah was born, Kat held him for two hours pressed against her chest. She had never felt so much love and pain intertwined into one. Then the nurses took him away, leaving Ryan and Kat devastated, sitting in a hospital room alone together, shattered. Kat had never cried so much in so little time. Although she was acquainted with grief, this was a whole new level. Her eyes were puffy and burned from the tears she had shed. Her body was so feeble the nurses had to physically place her in the wheelchair upon dismissal. Ryan was stoic, uncertain what to say or do. A piece of Kat left the hospital room that day when they took Noah out of her arms forever.

Ryan pushed Kat in the wheelchair to the car. Kat asked where Noah's car seat had gone. Ryan had made sure to remove the car seat before taking her down to the vehicle. He apprehensively told Kat he already had taken it out and placed it in the trunk. She realized Ryan did not have the words to soothe her or console her. He remained silent on the ride home. Tears ran down her cheeks, although she never said a word either. That day changed everything.

CHAPTER
FOUR

Nearly a year after the loss of Noah, Kat looked down at her cell phone. Amy was calling again. Kat answered the phone. Amy had already rung her twice that morning. Kat knew Amy would show up on her doorstep if she didn't answer. "Hey," Kat answered.

"Good morning," Amy said.

"Good morning, Amy."

"Got any plans for lunch today?"

"I don't feel well, Amy."

"Kat, we are having lunch today. You need to get out of that house."

She failed to mention to Amy that she was getting out, just not socially. She was secretly tracking her spouse's mistress. "Fine," Kat replied. "Where, and what time?" Kat rolled her eyes, as she knew Amy wouldn't accept a no today; she could tell in her voice she was determined.

"Meet me at eleven forty-five at Lindens."

Before Noah, Amy and Kat used to meet up for lunch frequently to discuss work and plans for weekends. After Kat was let go from the paper, Amy was promoted to editor in chief, and Kat knew it should have been her promotion. She was an extraordinary editor, and had Kat been more self-assured and ambitious, she could have chosen any editing job in New York City. She was not; she was apprehensive and scared of failure. And now she was failing, the very thing that frightened her.

When Kat arrived at Lindens for lunch, Amy was already there, waiting by the entrance. Amy hugged her tightly. "It's so good to see you out, Kat. I'm not going to lie to you: you don't look great."

"Thanks." As she sat, Kat glanced down at the menu, trying not to make eye contact with Amy. "How have you been?" Kat asked.

Amy started to talk about this and that, and Kat half listened, looking up once in a while so that Amy would think she was interested. Amy loved to talk, mostly about herself. She was a good friend to Kat, though; she cared sincerely about her. She never abandoned her, and she reached out reliably.

"Kat? What do you think?"

She was lost in her own thoughts. Sophia was on her mind. "I'm sorry—what?"

"Kat, did you even hear anything I said?"

"I'm sorry. I was trying to decide what I wanted to eat."

"Oh my God, Kat, get your shit together already. You have been through a lot, but it's time."

"Time for what?" Kat asked.

Amy hesitated. "Time to get your shit together," she said firmly. "It's been months, Kat. Almost a year." Amy shrugged.

Kat looked at her nails nervously. *Unkept,* she thought. *Maybe Amy is right.* She was lost in despair or obsession. On the days when she didn't follow the lovers, she was insignificant. She felt that each day was meaningless. Her constant had become traipsing around the city, trailing Ryan or Sophia. Some days

17

she didn't even eat. She would forget. She would wrap herself in Sophia and Ryan's daily tasks, surrendering her own.

Ryan had made it easy for Kat; he had hired Maria to keep the house. Kat would halfheartedly keep the laundry and, some days, would make the bed before Maria arrived. Maria arrived daily like clockwork. She spoke little English, although Kat appreciated that, for it meant she wouldn't want to strike up chatter or befriend Kat. Kat's only real responsibility was dredging herself out of bed to occasionally pick up dry cleaning or follow Sophia. Ryan had removed all accountability from Kat; he felt she was no longer capable. It was a good thing Ryan was wealthy; it handed Kat the ability to fade away and lose herself, just as she craved. Little did anyone know she did more than she let on. Either she was completely irrelevant to the world, or she was preoccupied with her husband and his lover. She went from one extreme to the other.

"So are you in?" Amy asked.

"In?"

"For the event." Amy rolled her eyes at Kat.

She once again had not heard a word Amy said.

"Everyone will be there. It's the annual charity ball. You can dress up and have a nice night out. God knows you and Ryan both need it. I'm certain he received an invitation."

Kat was certain he had too. She never opened the mail anymore; that was another of Ryan's duties. She knew Ryan was smart enough not to have anything involving his affair sent to their home, in case of possible accidental inspection. He got an invitation each year, and they had made appearances twice previously. The food was grand, and the attire was remarkable. You had to be someone significant to be given an invite, someone established. A thought raced through Kat's mind: Would Sophia be attending?

"I'll talk to Ryan. I'll think about it."

"Really?" Amy bounced in her chair with kid-like excitement, clapping her hands gently, as if she were about to blow out her candles and devour her birthday cake.

What the hell was Kat thinking? She had yet to face any of her friends or associates. Basically, she had yet to face the outside world at all. She also knew she was not runway ready; she had let herself go. She would have so much to do, including her hair. She hadn't had it colored in months, and the gray was prominent, even through the blonde. Kat used to be lovely. Not Megan Fox lovely—that was Sophia. Kat was simple, with pale, glass-like skin. It had no flaws but never appeared sun-kissed. She had shoulder-length dirty-blonde hair. She was pretty but simple. She was slender, not toned like Sophia. Kat's eyes were hazel. She was often compared to the British actress Rosamund Pike from *Gone Girl* but a shorter version. She didn't share the long legs that Rosamund had; she was lacking about two inches. On Kat's thirty-first birthday, Ryan had wrapped up the *Gone Girl* book as a joke for Kat, and as she'd ripped open the pale pink wrapping, they'd shared a belly laugh. She never had read the book. Shortly after, she had become pregnant with Noah, and the book had been shelved.

"We have three weeks, Kat. Don't flake on me, and Ryan will be thrilled you are even entertaining the idea of attending!"

Kat knew that wasn't true. Ryan seemed to have become comfortable with Kat in her current state. She assumed that made it easier for his new entertainment or exploits. He even occasionally encouraged her to rest or told her to take all the time she needed. *Thrilled* was not the word.

"He hasn't mentioned it to me, Amy."

"No, I'm sure he hasn't. Maybe he didn't want to put any

pressure on you. To be honest, I expected a no from you today. This will be good for you and Ryan."

Little did Amy know.

Kat went home. That evening, Ryan returned home, as he always did. That was comforting to Kat. She knew he would always come home—out of pity, but he came home. She had takeout delivered and ready upon his arrival. He had mentioned to her that he was grateful to have a meal after a long day of work, so she always made sure he did, even on her bad days. She didn't always join him, but the food was always there for him. She had joined him most nights for the last few weeks, aware that she was losing him to Sophia. It was her way of feeling somewhat empowered: sitting for dinner with him in Sophia's absence. Kat persuaded herself that alone was progress; she was unsuspectingly fighting for what rightfully belonged to her: Ryan. Ryan was oblivious to her revelation, as she kept quiet about the affair.

Again, she sat across from him at the exquisite dinner table they'd had shipped from Europe after his promotion, and she watched him while he ate. She wondered if he had seen Sophia that day. She had not followed either one of them that day, due to her lunch date. She still had days when she did not get out of bed; however, if she did, it was most certainly to observe and spy.

"I had lunch with Amy today," she said.

He looked at her, surprised. "You did? That's great, Kat."

Kat was sure he was unaware of what her days even consisted of at that point. "Yes, it was nice. It felt good. We went to Lindens and then went to some boutiques near there."

He looked almost puzzled. "I didn't realize you were feeling better."

She wanted to scream out, "Of course you wouldn't notice;

you are too busy fucking your girlfriend!" but she didn't. She softly responded, "I believe I am."

It was clear to Kat that Ryan had checked out. He failed to notice her at all. He didn't notice her presence as she sat in front of him, frantically trying, attempting to rebuild herself and repair herself, trying to win him back in some fashion. She had begun to engage more often and ask questions about work when he got home. She dressed up and put on makeup most days, at least before he arrived home or after her secret spy outings. She even occasionally brushed her hand or her body against his in the kitchen. She pressed her feet against him in the bed here and there or inched closer to him while he slept. Kat was making small efforts to try to get his attention. Unfortunately, it was only when she discovered Sophia that she began these antics, deciding to try to save her marriage, and by that time, Sophia was already in the driver's seat.

"Amy mentioned the annual charity ball is coming up. Are we attending this year?" Kat muttered.

Ryan set his wineglass down. "Kat, what? I was under the impression you were not up for a social event. You have been in this house for months, barely speaking a word to me, barely leaving this house, and now you want to attend the ball?" He looked confused.

She just sat in silence, unsure how to respond. She was always careful in the way she responded to Ryan. That was one thing he had always appreciated about her, or so he had said in the past. He said she was always thoughtful in her choice of tone and words, and he was grateful for it. She was always sensible, graceful, and soft. Now she sensed those responses only annoyed him. He would stare at her with annoyance in his eyes. His body language was tense and uneasy toward her. He would cross his arms across his chest and wait impatiently. She wondered if he thought she was ingenuine. Did he want fire from her, a reaction like Sophia would give? But he was unwilling to draw it out of her. She was right: he had checked out.

"Amy thinks it would be good for me. For us," she said.

He stood with his plate in hand and left the room without a word.

CHAPTER
FIVE

Ryan used to laugh with Kat. She realized she hadn't seen him laugh in some time. In fact, she hadn't seen him smile since they lost Noah—not at her at least. She had witnessed him smile at Sophia many times. Every time struck her in the gut. She believed that smile belonged to her. It often sent Kat into a panic; she would lose her breath. She longed to feel something— anything. She had succumbed to the numbness, an emptiness, until she began following them. Following them made her feel something. It was anger, but it was a feeling. She needed it.

She would picture herself walking right up to them and confronting them together courageously, taking back her territory, but she never did. She watched them, time after time, smile, laugh, and brush skin across the table or playfully beneath the table. She knew which hotel was their spot, where they met to make love. The thought made Kat sick, disgusted, jealous, infuriated, and sad. She would sit there across the street, waiting for them to reappear, feeling desperate and dreading the next time. She would bite her nails to nubs, usually drawing blood. She would nervously pace and occasionally throw up. She felt embarrassed, asking herself why she would subject herself to the details of it all. It always came, the next time, not to her surprise. Other days she blamed herself and questioned his conduct, almost arguing with herself as if it were her fault: *What else was Ryan to do? Wait around for me to slip out of my stupor? Was he going to leave me? No, he wouldn't. He loves me.* At least she had convinced herself he did.

They had been through so much; he would never leave. Kat had helped Ryan take care of his mother before she passed. His mother had loved Kat as her own. Kat had been supportive of Ryan while he climbed his own ladder to success. She had taken care of him. She was a caregiver naturally. She always had put Ryan's needs above her own while managing to maintain her own career. Back then, she would have never allowed Maria to man her home; she could handle it. He knew that, and he often thanked her with gifts or trips. Ryan enjoyed traveling, whereas Kat was a homebody but always managed to have a delightful time. They had been close—inseparable. In love, she knew he'd adored coming home to Kat and spending hours discussing the day and the future, sharing thoughts, and making love. Many good memories would surface, and in those moments, while watching them, she missed her old life.

The next morning, Kat awoke before Ryan, which was unusual. She had lain in bed awake for hours that night, convincing herself to get her shit together, so she got up and made her husband breakfast.

"You made breakfast?"

"I did. Your favorite: omelets," Kat replied.

"Kat, I'm sorry, but I have an early meeting. I don't have time. I didn't hear you get up."

"You looked peaceful. I didn't want to disturb you," she said while filling his coffee mug.

"Thank you." He reached for his coffee. "Listen, I have to go." He made eye contact with her briefly. "Have a good day, OK? I'll see you this evening."

"You too," she replied as he walked out the door.

Kat opted not to follow Ryan or Sophia that day. She knew time was running out, and her last conversation with Amy kept ringing in her ears. *Get your shit together.* If she really wanted to save her marriage, she had to start somewhere. Today she would begin. When she had lost Noah, she had also lost herself. Sadly, the motivation for restoring herself was winning back her husband and taking back her life. She had work to do.

She called Amy to discuss the charity ball details, and she fired Maria in the meantime. She told Maria she no longer needed her services. She sent her on her way with a generous severance. She was going to take back her house, herself, and her man.

"I need my hair done, Amy. I can't go like this."

Amy screeched, "I'm so proud of you! Finally, some energy in your voice. I'll make a call to my girl; she owes me a favor. I really think this is a step in the right direction for you."

Kat was excited for the first time in a long time. She had decided the night before, after meeting with Amy, that it was time to rejoin society. She hoped it wasn't too late. She had bargained with herself. She was not letting Noah go; she was healing. She was no good like this. She was exhausted of feeling lost. Noah would understand. She had mourned for so long— long enough to let her marriage slip through her fingers. It was time to regain control of her emotions and rebuild what she had neglected for some time: her partner, Ryan.

Ryan met Sophia for lunch—a normal occurrence.

"You've barely touched your lunch, Ryan. What's wrong?" Sophia asked.

He knew he wasn't himself; he was distracted.

"Is it work?" she asked.

He didn't reply; he just stared at his salad, lost in thought.

"Ryan?" she said.

He looked up at her. "She wants to go to the charity ball."

"Who?" Sophia asked.

"Kat." He paused. "She told me last night she's beginning to feel better."

Ryan knew Sophia wasn't like Kat; she said what she felt and not so gracefully at times.

"What the fuck does that mean, Ryan? You're considering taking her?"

Ryan grew anxious. He began to fidget in his chair, uncrossing his legs. He was aware that Sophia was used to getting her way. Her looks made it easy for her. She was used to being in charge and being able to control most situations. Ryan knew most women found her intimidating and threatening. Sophia was blunt and honest, and usually, that was attractive to him. She didn't typically think before she spoke. She had confided in him, divulging details of her life to him. She had grown up in Madrid, and he had come to the conclusion she always had been fancied there, as she was exceptionally beautiful and intelligent. Her parents had sent her to the States for college with money they had inherited. She'd received her bachelor's degree in criminal justice before applying for law school. She had been social in college, the typical sorority girl, and partied—the opposite of Kat. She loved to parade around New York and was considered a socialite. She and Ryan excused their behavior as business, although people were suspicious.

"Sophia, I don't know. She's my wife. I can't very well refuse to bring her."

Stunned, she scooted back her chair and placed her napkin on the table. "That's fine, Ryan. Take your wife." She stood assertively, grabbed her Chanel bag, and left without saying goodbye.

Ryan was slightly relieved.

After she abruptly exited, Ryan called her four times before she answered. "Sophia, please just talk to me."

"What is there to talk about? Are we going to discuss Kat and how you can't leave her, because she has no one? The whole sad story on repeat? I'm sick of that conversation, Ryan. I guess you're sleeping with her again too now that she is feeling better?"

"No, I'm not. Sophia, please stop. You know how difficult this is for me. You knew the situation."

"Fuck the situation. Do you still love her?"

"I don't know," he replied. Silence filled the line. She hung up the phone.

"I'm here. Just pulled up," Kat said before hanging up the phone. She walked into Bergdorf's.

"You're late." Amy rolled her eyes.

Amy had arranged for a personal stylist to help them search for the perfect evening gowns. Kat wasn't even sure she was going to the ball but needed the distraction. She wanted to attend, but Ryan had not mentioned it. She was confused about how the conversation had ended a few days ago. She did not reveal that to Amy, however; she only pretended she was going. Sensing that Amy was proud of her, Kat couldn't rain on her parade today.

It was a good day. Amy deliberately tried on some horrendous dresses to make Kat laugh, and she did. Kat laughed, and it felt good. Kat was trying to divert herself from wondering if Ryan had seen Sophia that day, so Amy's actions were perfect. Amy bought a stunning black dress that fit her figure well. Amy loved to show off her figure; although she was slightly overweight, she felt comfortable in her own skin, and Kat loved that about Amy. Kat decided to look around before buying a dress that day. Amy agreed to go another day to explore more dresses elsewhere.

Kat hurried home, intending to beat Ryan home to prepare dinner. He never asked about Maria. She found that odd. She decided Maria had called Ryan, and he'd chalked it up to her feeling better. She would have appreciated a word of encouragement, however. They had tiptoed around conversation for so long it was difficult to learn how to communicate again. She poured a glass of chardonnay and prepped her stir fry. Ryan should arrive home shortly, she knew. She planned on bringing up the ball again and quietly pleading with him to take her. She wanted to be on his arm. She wanted him to see her dressed up. She wanted to prove to him she was capable of being sexy again.

Maybe. She would try her best. She also knew Sophia would more than likely be a guest.

Ryan arrived home. He seemed slightly flustered. He entered and threw his laptop down onto the entrance table, along with his keys.

"Hi there." She smiled.

He appeared caught off guard. "Hi." He gave her a slight smile.

She loved his smile. It was something. He could get into a lot of trouble with a smile like that, and he could also get himself out of trouble with it. She walked right up to him and kissed his lips softly. He didn't kiss her back. She drew no attention to it and walked away. "Dinner is ready when you are."

He stood motionless, seemingly taken aback and confused. She returned to the kitchen. He soon followed. He had removed his suit and put on an old Bon Jovi T-shirt. They had bought the T-shirt together at a concert they'd crashed. He knew someone who'd let them in without charge, although Ryan could afford it. They'd wanted to feel risqué and do something crazy. It had been the first time Kat smoked marijuana—and the last. They'd had so much fun that night at the concert, being carefree, dancing, drinking, and getting high on life and weed. Ryan was always able to pull out the mischievous, less-reserved Kat.

Ryan looked tired. He sat, rubbing his hands together as if he were nervous. "Kat, I've been thinking about the charity ball."

She turned around and set the stir fry on the table. "Yeah?"

"You feel certain you are ready for this? There will be questions. Kat, you dropped off the face of the earth. People will ask where you have been, and people will ask you about Noah. Are you prepared for that?"

She slowly sat and placed her napkin in her lap. Before

answering, she made his plate and hers. "Grief never ends; it changes. Ryan, the death of Noah altered my being, my soul. I can't apologize for it. I'm learning life will go on; it will just never be the same. Am I prepared? No, I am not. But I am beginning to heal."

That night was a little different from most nights. They sat at the table for hours, talking. Although they held only small talk, it was a little victory for Kat.

"Remember the time we missed our flight home from Fiji, and I cried in the airport?" she asked with a smile. "I remember thinking that was a devastating circumstance." She paused before she continued. "Looking back, that was silly of me to think," she said as she reminisced.

As he sipped another drink from his glass, he smiled. "Yeah, those were the good ole days, weren't they? We sat in that airport on standby for two days. It wasn't that bad, now that I think about it." He twisted his napkin in his hand with a deep-rooted look upon his face, as if he were lost in thought. "Kat, we have had some good times, haven't we?"

The next morning, Ryan left for work. Kat had a self-care day planned. The previous evening and her chat with Ryan had motivated her. She had to pry herself away from Sophia; she had to free herself from the obsession she had developed. She would fight and resist the urge at all cost. She did not want Sophia to have that hold on her one day longer.

After coffee on the rooftop, she watered her plants. She took in her view. It was magical. Ryan had been so proud the day he moved her into their new home in Chelsea. It was a lovely penthouse with four bedrooms and plenty of space for a nursery and her gardening. He had made sure to have someone build her custom raised beds for all her flowers and the small garden she always had wanted.

She did two loads of laundry before making her bed and leaving the house. The sun was bright, but the air was crisp and cool. She loved the smell of the city and the sounds. She was amazed at the way the city never slept. The subways, the buzzing of the streets, and even the obnoxious sound of the horns brought her comfort. The city never failed. It was strong, undefeated. Her favorite place was Central Park, near the heart of Manhattan. She and Ryan used to venture there regularly and spend the whole day. *Not today, Kat*, she told herself. She was on a mission—no diversions.

She hailed a cab and ventured toward East Twenty-Third. Amy had arranged for Kat to have her hair colored and cut. She felt pleased with herself in that moment. She was rescuing herself, reacquainting her feet with the earth beneath her.

When her hair was done, she didn't recognize herself. She examined herself in the mirror and silently whispered, "I look good, damn it."

Kat had not touched Ryan in five months, and they had not had sex in six months. *No wonder he strayed. Tonight is the night.* She was going to make her move. The thought made her palms sweat. She hurried home.

CHAPTER
SEVEN

Sophia waited impatiently for Ryan to call. It had been four days since he had called her and even longer since they had made love. She was outraged, and she was jealous. The emotion felt unfamiliar to her. She had left a message inviting him to her apartment. They never met at her apartment; it was not convenient for either of them during the week. She was frantic. She had to see him that weekend. Ryan was hers. She had claimed him, and she always got what she wanted. Sophia had fallen in love. She had never been in love. She craved him. Sophia had been promiscuous before Ryan, but he was different. Sophia had abandoned all plans for the weekend. Her plans had changed. She headed to Ryan's. It didn't take her long to make the trip from NoHo to Chelsea. She watched tolerantly, waiting for Ryan. She continued to ring his phone, but each time, the call went to voice mail. *How dare he.* She felt used and neglected.

Kat arrived home. Sophia had never seen Kat in person before; she had only seen pictures of Kat after stalking the newspaper she used to work for. Kat didn't have social media. Sophia never really had felt the need to stalk her; she had always felt she was winning—until now. Kat was prettier than Sophia remembered. She was elegant and looked well put together—nothing like Sophia had envisioned in her mind.

Ryan arrived home shortly after Kat. Sophia watched. She never called to Ryan; she just surveyed. Ryan looked as if he had been to the gym. *Since when does he go to the gym on a Saturday?* she asked herself. She knew his schedule. He typically went in the evenings after having dinner with Kat and either returned to his office to work or met Sophia. He often used the gym as an excuse to get out of the house to meet her. More rage filled her head. What was happening? She was losing control.

They reemerged. Kat was wearing a black plunge midi dress that hugged her body just right and heels. Ryan wore a gray Tom Ford suit Sophia had removed from his body more than once. He was taking Kat out.

After their night out, Ryan watched as Kat sat at her vanity, removing her makeup from the evening. He had taken her to the grand opening of a new restaurant not far from their home. The new chef was from the United Kingdom, and Ryan and Kat had decided he lived up to his name. The food had been magnificent. Throughout the evening, they'd caught up like old friends, and the dialogue had flowed effortlessly. They'd laughed and flirted even. As they'd walked out of the restaurant, Ryan had grabbed Kat's hand. His grip, gentle and soft, had sent a shock through Kat's body. The night had reminded Kat of many dates before their downfall, before they'd disengaged. Maybe they'd needed a reminder of how easily and naturally they could connect with each other. If she had mourned alongside him, if she had allowed him to lean on her, and if she had leaned on him, would things have been different for them? Would he have surrendered to infidelity? She had an infinite amount of memories to prove they had been happy once.

"Your hair looked great this evening." He had noticed she had it colored and styled. He hadn't seen her like that in so long. He had forgotten how beautiful he thought she was. She was naturally lovely.

"Thank you," Kat replied as she peered back at him in the mirror.

"Kat," he said, "I'm sorry." He was sincere.

They continued to make eye contact. Neither one looked away. Kat didn't reply; she rose from her vanity and moved toward Ryan. He was propped on the edge of the bed. He looked sad, with guilt in his eyes. She knew why. She kissed him. It was a kiss filled with all the words she didn't say. They made love that night twice. It felt like old times.

The next morning, Ryan woke up to four new voice mails. He suspected they were from Sophia. He had not called her in five days. He was confused and avoiding Sophia. He had made it clear in the beginning that he could not leave Kat, as she was fragile. She had already endured so much pain—her parents, her grandparents, Eve, Noah. He could not be responsible for another loss. He and Sophia had had multiple conversations about it, especially on days when Sophia was restless and urging him to leave her. She occasionally behaved erratically, throwing tantrums. She could be unpredictable. She had once thrown her cell phone so hard at his windshield that the glass cracked, and her cell phone shattered. He was infatuated with her even still. She had a fire inside her she wouldn't apologize for. She feared nothing; she was a force. It was sexy. She knew how to handle Ryan and how to touch him. She was poised and determined, leaving him wanting more each time.

"Sophia," he mumbled as she answered her cell.

"Where the hell have you been? I've been calling for days," she said. Her voice was quivering.

"I can't do this right now. We can meet later this week and talk, OK?" he responded.

She began to cry.

"Please don't cry." He longed for words to relieve her, but he had none. He knew nothing he could say would change the outcome. They decided to meet on Monday. He owed her that much.

Monday morning came too quickly for Kat. Ryan and Kat spent the majority of the weekend in bed, wrapped tightly around each other. It had been years since they shared a weekend like that. Kat never once thought about Sophia. She focused on Ryan. It wasn't about fixing a broken marriage; it was about building a new one. For once in her life, she felt brave and assured. She chose to move forward. She forgave Ryan that weekend. She wasn't the only one who'd lost Noah, and she came to terms with that. He had been alone in his grief because she'd pulled away from him—from everyone.

Before leaving for work, Ryan kissed her forehead. "I enjoyed this weekend," he said as he grinned at her and closed the door behind him.

She had a complete day ahead of her. She was picking up her dress for the charity event that weekend and had to deliver Ryan's tuxedo to the cleaners. She was meeting Amy for lunch, and then they were heading across town for manicures.

EIGHT

"Can you believe Tom? What an asshole!" Amy ranted. She had caught him sending his secretary inappropriate text messages and thrown him out. "You're lucky, Kat. You got the last good one."

Kat felt a sudden wave of sickness. She had never told Amy. She was embarrassed and ashamed. Amy had a bad streak with men. She was enticed by toxic men. Tom loved women and had a wandering eye, and everyone noticed but Amy. She and Tom had been on and off for years. The news didn't surprise Kat; it wasn't his first offense. She listened as Amy fumed.

Ryan made his way to lunch and tensely waited for Sophia. Sophia was never late; she was punctual. He wondered if she was standing him up, proving a point. That was something she would have done. It was 11:17, and they'd agreed to meet at 11:00. He glanced out the window. She was crossing the street, heading toward the diner. He noticed she was wearing sunglasses and carrying her umbrella. There was a drizzle of light rain, and it was overcast, so why was she wearing sunglasses?

She trudged in and sat. Her posture was different, and she was unkempt. She rooted around in her purse and pulled out her phone. They sat in silence for what felt like five minutes. It was evident when she removed her sunglasses she had been crying. He felt anxious, and he did not want to provoke her. "I don't want to hurt you, Sophia," he said, and a single tear rolled down her cheek. "I can't stand to see you this way."

She interrupted him. "I'm pregnant, Ryan!" she shouted as her hand hit the table.

Ryan sat stunned. He cupped a hand over his mouth before replying. "Are you certain?"

"Of course I'm certain, Ryan," she said as she grabbed a napkin from the table to wipe her face.

Ryan was in shock. He wanted children still but not like this. *With a mistress?* What would people think? What about Kat? And his mother? *She would not be proud of any of this.* He began to question everything. He had made a mess of things. He felt sick. He left a hundred-dollar bill on the table and rose from his seat. "I have to go. I'm sorry, Sophia." The news definitely had thrown a curveball into a nonexistent plan.

Ryan left the diner, still feeling sick and light-headed. Sophia had told him she was on birth control. He never had used protection. He'd trusted her. The news would kill Kat. She couldn't find out. He would make sure of it. He wasn't in love with Sophia; he never had felt the deep connection he and Kat shared. It was sex. It was lust. She was exciting, but this was too much. He needed to clear his head so he could figure out what to do. Ryan returned to work briefly only to head home. He needed to lie down to shut off the world, if only momentarily.

Ryan headed home. He arrived home to Kat on the computer.

"Hey, you're home early." She looked puzzled. "Is everything OK?" He didn't appear OK.

"Yeah, I'm fine. Are you working on your résumé?" he asked, clearly deliberately changing the subject.

She turned back toward the computer screen. "Oh yeah, I don't know. I'm entertaining the idea of working again. What do you think?" He was reading something on his phone when she turned back around. "Ryan, is everything OK?"

"Yes, I'm sorry. What were you saying?"

She knew he was lying. He always cleared his throat and slightly tilted his head back when he lied. He wasn't OK. His face was flushed, and he was tense.

His phone rang. "I'm sorry, but I need to take this." He marched upstairs.

Kat followed him quietly. She wondered if he was talking to Sophia. Kat convinced herself into believing he was ending things with her after the week they had shared. Things had felt so normal, like they used to. She pressed her ear against the bedroom door.

"I can't talk right now. Please just give me some time," he said.

It was her. He was talking to Sophia.

"I'm not saying that. I just need some time, OK? I have to go. I'll come by tomorrow."

He will come by tomorrow? Why? Why does he need to come by? She felt her blood pressure rising as she tiptoed back downstairs.

Ryan didn't come back downstairs until dinner. He had showered, and his eyes were bloodshot.

Has he been crying? she asked herself.

Talk was minimal that evening. He was invested in something else, and she intended to figure out what.

CHAPTER
NINE

Amy called bright and early the next morning. Kat had tossed and turned all night. Ryan had poured himself three glasses of whiskey after dinner, which Kat knew was his drink of choice when he was anxious.

"Good morning, sunshine!" Amy said cheerfully.

"Good morning, Amy. It's a little early, don't you think?"

"Not for the working woman," Amy said sarcastically.

She was always a smart-ass. Kat didn't usually mind it, but she was a little irritated by it that morning.

"Anyway," Amy said, "I have to come that way to pick up Tom's tux around lunch. Want to meet at Lindens for a bite?"

Kat was confused. "Wait—Tom's tux?"

"Turns out they weren't sleeping together; they are just friends," Amy said.

Kat didn't have the energy to debate with Amy that morning. "Great. I'm sorry, but I can't have lunch; I have too much to do today. Maybe tomorrow?" Kat was debating tailing Sophia that day. She needed to know if her husband had broken things off or if he was still seeing her.

Amy began rambling about work and how tomorrow she had a list of things to get done.

"Another day then," Kat said, interrupting her.

"OK. If not, then I will see you later this week at the charity ball," Amy said. She hung up.

Finally. Kat adored Amy, but today she had other things on her mind. Ryan had left extra early, and she wondered if it was because he hadn't wanted to face her that morning. Something was happening.

Ryan had left the house that morning and headed to Sophia's place. She had already called that morning. She had told him she had every intention of keeping the baby and blathered on and on about having a family. He knew she didn't want to be a mother; she was only used to getting her way. She wanted to win. It wasn't about the baby; it was about him. He was clued into her manipulation techniques by now. He was angry, mainly at himself for trusting her. His only solution for the moment was to appease Sophia and keep her happy for now so she didn't do anything crazy or impulsive. She tended to emotionally react, and he was worried she would divulge their secret to someone, Kat in particular. Thoughts had raced through his mind all night about his marriage, his reputation, and his fortune. All were at stake. He knew the situation could get out of control quickly. Kat could afford a high-powered divorce attorney provided to her with his money. Given the situation, she might take more than half.

He thought about Kat. This would destroy her. She had lost Noah, and now he was expecting a baby with another woman. And he could not shake the feeling that his mother undeniably would have been disappointed in him.

After hearing Ryan's conversation previously, Kat decided to investigate that day. Was the affair really over, or was she living on false hope? Was she that desperate to believe the last few days meant everything was back on track? Was she that naive?

Sophia never arrived for her usual morning coffee run. Kat was planted on her usual bench, reading the *New York Times*. She often wondered when Sophia actually worked. How was she so accomplished while still finding time to keep up with new trends? Kat had decided Sophia was not nearly as good at her job as she was made out to be. She would sit there and watch Sophia have her coffee and scroll on her phone. Sometimes a friend would join Sophia. They would laugh and catch up, unaware of Kat's intrusion. That day, Sophia didn't show. Kat took the subway to Hall and Associates, and she waited. Sophia never left for lunch, nor did she leave that late afternoon. She never went to work.

Kat made her way to NoHo, to Sophia's. It was dark; she knew Ryan would beat her home. What was she doing there? Why had Ryan agreed to meet Sophia that day? What was her plan? She saw no movement and no lights. Maybe he just needed to meet her face-to-face to break up with her—that would have been the gentlemanly way to do it. Ryan was always a noble man—or he used to be.

Kat decided to head home. She stood from the bench to head toward the station. Realizing she'd forgotten her bag, she turned back to retrieve it from the bench. *Amy?* She spotted Amy walking out of Sophia's apartment building. What was Amy doing there? Did she know Sophia? Whom did she know in Sophia's building? Kat thought about calling out to her but decided against it, as she would have had no answer as to why she was there herself. She remained frozen, confused. She watched as Amy darted around the corner, disappearing into the night. Kat caught the subway home, even more perplexed.

To Kat's surprise, she beat her husband home. She tried to call his cell. There was no answer; the call was sent to voice mail. "Hey, Ryan, just, um, checking on you. Call me back. I love you."

It was late. She fled to the rooftop, grabbing an unopened bottle of wine on the way up. She would visit the rooftop to think; the lights and the sounds of the city calmed her. She made her way to the bar and uncorked the wine. She had begun drinking more often since discovering her husband had a lover. On many days, she felt angry, while on others, she believed she was the one responsible. It frustrated her. Some days she was bitter, and other days she had no energy to care.

She began thinking about Amy. Amy was a faithful and loyal friend, always there for Kat. She had been ecstatic when she found out Kat was pregnant with Noah. She'd hosted a shower and even helped prepare the nursery. Kat wondered if Amy had ever run into Sophia. Why had she been exiting her building? Amy was friendly and had a wide array of friends. Kat couldn't keep up with her social circle or her boyfriends. Tom was the most consistent, although they had a vicious cycle of calling it quits, always followed by reconnecting. Kat believed Amy had a fear of dying alone.

Kat finished the bottle with no sign of Ryan. She was curled up in a blanket, gazing up at the stars, hardly awake, wondering where her husband was.

The cold air hit her face like a brick, waking her. She grabbed her cell to check the time. It was 1:47, and she had received no calls from Ryan. She unwrapped herself from her blanket. *Two blankets?* He had come home and placed an extra blanket on her to keep her warm. He must have. She sped downstairs into the house. There he lay, asleep in their bed. She started to wake him but decided against it. She was confused. She tiptoed out, made her way to the guest bedroom, and lay there until morning.

Morning came. Kat peeked through the blinds; it was overcast and dreary outside. *Perfect day for it,* she thought. She heard Ryan stirring but decided to hide away in the guest bedroom, afraid of tension. She didn't have the courage to race in there and ask him where he had been and why he had not called her. She did what she always did—kept quiet—unwilling to rock the boat. No wonder he felt secure in having an affair, she thought; she never questioned him. She never felt the need to. Her head hurt, and she suspected the bottle of wine she'd gulped down the night before, or was it anxiety she was feeling in the moment?

Ryan peeked through the slightly ajar door, and they made eye contact. He opened the door and sat on the end of the bed. He looked beat and tattered, although he was dressed in a suit and ready for work. The suit couldn't cover up the circles under his eyes. He spoke first. "I'm sorry about last night."

She waited for him to continue, still keeping eye contact.

"I went to Mom's grave. I should have called. I didn't realize how long I was there. Kat, I'm sorry." He stood and moved closer to her. He bent over and kissed her cheek. "I'll see you tonight."

She ignored her gut instinct to scream and curse at him and confront him; instead, she smiled. He walked out the door. She never said a word. She wondered if he was telling the truth. She hated that she no longer trusted him. Kat lay there in bed, debating her next step.

Kat lay there for most of the morning, trying to get a grip. Her phone rang. "Hello?"

"Hello. This is Martin Merrill with *New York Daily Magazine*. Am I speaking with Mrs. Katherine Letty?"

"Yes, this is she. Hello, Mr. Merrill," she said.

"Afternoon. I'm calling regarding your résumé you recently submitted to our magazine, in the chance you are still interested."

Wow, she thought, *I just sent that out yesterday.* She stuttered, "Yes, yes, I am interested. Thank you."

"Great. I was hoping so. At your convenience, of course, would you come by the *Daily* to sit down to discuss moving forward?"

She paused momentarily. Her head was pounding from the night before. "Absolutely. How does this afternoon sound?" She decided she needed the distraction.

Her first thought was to call Ryan, as she usually shared these moments with him, but she didn't. She jumped out of bed, looking forward to her meeting and forgetting her headache.

Kat dressed in high-waisted black pants with a bow-neck blush silk blouse. She felt strong and self-assured as she hailed a cab to the *Daily*.

"I'm here to meet Martin Merrill. Katherine Letty," Kat told the receptionist.

"Mr. Merrill will be with you shortly. Please take a seat," she said in a firm tone.

"Of course." Kat turned and sat. The room was modern and sharp, and remarkable art hung from the walls. Unexpectedly, the seats were comfortable. A plethora of issues of *New York Daily Magazine* were displayed on every table.

"Mrs. Letty, please follow me."

She followed the receptionist down a long hallway to what appeared to be a conference room.

"Mr. Merrill will be joining you momentarily. May I get you something to drink? Coffee? Water?"

"Oh no, I'm fine. Thank you." Kat sat alone in the conference room for what felt like forever, thinking about how uncomfortable she felt. She had spent so little time in the last year communicating with others it almost felt foreign. The only person she really had conversations with was Amy, and usually, Amy did all the talking.

The door opened, and two gentlemen walked through the door. Kat stood, and they shook hands.

"Hello, Katherine. I'm Martin Merrill, and this is Baron Marco, our managing editor."

"Nice to meet you both," Kat replied.

Martin was the editor in chief. Kat had done a little research before submitting her application previously. Baron was attractive and much older than Kat. Baron was tall—six foot two or so, she guessed—and had dark skin and salt-and-pepper hair, with a beard to match. She assumed his hair had been jet black before the gray. The gray was sophisticated and mature. He had a sharp jawline chiseled to perfection and darting dark brown eyes that sent Kat into overdrive, unintentionally radiating sexuality.

Kat began blushing, and she could feel the warmth exuding from her cheeks. *Snap out of it, Kat. Jesus.*

Martin spoke. "Katherine, we can cut right to the chase. We know your work. You have quite a reputation. We are looking for an executive director."

She was amazed. They knew her reputation. She had a reputation. She was always critical of herself. *It's like riding a bike, right?* she told herself. "Let's discuss details," she said with authority.

CHAPTER
TEN

Ryan was home early. His tuxedo was hanging in the laundry room. *Shit, I forgot to pick my dress up from alterations.* The charity event was in two days. "Ryan?" she called. She walked up to the rooftop; he was perched on the side, staring at the city.

"It's a great view, isn't it, Kat?" he asked. He had a strange look about him. She didn't acknowledge the comment.

"You're home early," she said.

"Yeah, I feel terrible about last night. I thought maybe I could take you out for dinner." He looked back her.

What if she was wrong? What if he had ended it with Sophia, and Kat was silently punishing him after she had decided to forgive him? She was jumping to conclusions, acting on emotions.

"That sounds great. Let me change, and I'll meet you downstairs."

Her phone rang. It was Amy. "Hello?" Kat answered.

"Hey, I had a few minutes and wanted to see how your dress fit," Amy said.

"Actually, I was planning to pick it up tomorrow," Kat lied.

"Oh, I thought you had said today. Anyway, dinner plans?"

"Ryan and I are going out for dinner tonight. Not sure where yet."

"Oh, I know a place you have to try! It's amazing. You two will love it. It's a new robata grill next to the Swimming Pig Pub. What time? I'll meet you two there. I have to finish up a few things here, and I can catch up in a bit."

"Well, OK. Six is good. Text me the info."

They hung up. Amy was notorious for being intrusive. Kat thought, *Ryan won't be pleased.* He tolerated Amy. He always said she talked too much and wore out her welcome at times. Kat supposed Amy was just trying to be a good friend after Kat hit rock bottom. Kat was relieved; Amy's presence meant she wouldn't have to face reality and discuss the night before with Ryan. Expressing dissatisfaction or unhappiness was not Kat's strong suit. She was a go-with-the-flow, fall-in-line type of girl.

They met Amy at Tei Bans, the new Japanese restaurant Amy had raved about. Amy arrived at 6:14—late, as usual. Kat observed that Ryan was displeased with her intrusion. He had obviously planned on a romantic makeup dinner. She could tell he instantaneously became uptight; his face turned red, and his legs and arms appeared to stiffen. Awkwardly, the evening proceeded. They sat at a corner table near the restrooms. *An escape if needed*, Kat thought.

Amy sat. "Well, the ambience is nice, right? The food is even better. Hello, Ryan. How have you been?" Amy cast him a side look.

"Great, Amy. So glad you could join us," he said with sarcasm.

Amy failed to notice. "Have you two ordered drinks?"

Just as Kat started to answer, she saw him across the room, making his way toward her: Baron.

"Katherine Letty, twice in one day. What are the odds?" Baron smiled.

Kat felt weak in the knees even sitting. Her breath was taken away as if she had just plunged down a hill on a roller coaster. Was she nervous about being outed about her new job, or was it Baron himself who made her nervous? She wasn't sure.

"Hello, Mr. Marco. The odds apparently are favorable. Nice to see you again. This is my husband, Ryan, and my friend Amy Harris."

Ryan stood to shake hands, saying hello, and Amy looked up and smiled flirtatiously. "Does Mr. Marco have a first name?" Amy asked.

"Baron." He smiled as he reached out a hand to Amy.

Ryan sat back down in his chair.

Baron looked at Ryan. "We are thrilled to have Katherine coming to work with us. She will be just the addition we need at the *Daily*."

Ryan immediately cut his eyes at Kat. "Yes, indeed she will be." He looked back at Baron.

"Working with you at the *Daily*?" Amy asked, puzzled.

Kat said, "Yes, I've accepted a position there. Well, today, in fact. I was going to tell you tonight." The table was silent for a few seconds.

"I apologize, Katherine," Baron said. "It seems I've ruined your announcement."

Kat was blushing. "No need for apologies, Mr. Marco." She glanced at Amy.

"I'd best let you all get back to your evening. It was a pleasure to meet you two. Katherine, I will see you Monday." Baron made his way to the restroom.

Kat could feel Ryan and Amy staring at her. "Well, surprise," she said delicately.

Ryan remained quiet.

"Kat, the *Daily*? Wow. I mean, you didn't tell me you were thinking about going back to work," Amy said.

Kat looked at Ryan. "I mentioned it to Ryan just a few days ago, and well, it all happened so quickly. I'm very excited."

Thankfully, Amy began rambling about the ball that weekend, and the new job was old news instantly.

After dinner, when their Uber arrived, Ryan and Kat jumped in, and there was silence for the entire ride home. Kat wanted to apologize, but she hesitated. She grabbed his hand, and he reciprocated. She wasn't sure if he was annoyed or hurt. She knew she should have told him earlier. She had intended to tell him that evening. They arrived home, Ryan opened the door for Kat, and they went inside.

"An eventful evening that was, Katherine," he said.

She felt the sarcasm in his tone. "I was planning on telling you tonight at dinner. What do you think?"

"I think it would have been nice if I had heard it from my wife," he smugly replied.

"I'm sorry. That was embarrassing. I accepted a position as the executive director just today. I have been feeling more like myself again lately, and I think this is just what I need. This clearly wasn't something I intended on keeping a secret."

"Congratulations, Kat. I think it's great. I really do. I was only caught off guard," he said as he poured a glass of whiskey. He raised his glass. "Let's celebrate."

She poured herself a glass of chardonnay. "Cheers," she said as their glasses tapped gently.

Ryan hoisted her onto the counter and forcefully removed her thong. Her hands clawed his biceps as he thrust into her there on the counter. He was different—hostile. As he continued, Kat found herself lost in thought with Baron. Why was she thinking of Baron? What was going on? She felt guilty.

CHAPTER

ELEVEN

Kat woke the next morning. Ryan had left for work already and had left a note by the coffee maker: "I'll be home late. Have a good day." She thought about Sophia. Was he seeing her? Was he working? She decided she didn't have time to think about that today; she had plans. She needed to pick up her gown and run a few errands.

Ryan thought about Sophia on his way to work. It had been two days since he'd seen or spoken to her. Their last conversation had not ended well. She'd threatened to tell his wife she was carrying his baby. She was vicious and enraged. He'd tried bargaining with her. She wasn't ready to have a child and be a mother. Her career had taken off, and she was thriving. She definitely could not handle being a single mother, he had decided.

As for Kat, he was still shocked at the incident the night before. She never made impulsive decisions. Before Noah, they had told each other everything and discussed big decisions with each other. He thought her accepting a job without telling him was out of character for her. Kat was easy, not like Sophia. She was reasonable and responsible. She never would have deceived him, lying about birth control and becoming pregnant without regard to his feelings. Noah had been planned and expected.

Kat picked up the gown. It fit flawlessly. She was pleased. She picked up her cell and phoned Amy.

"Hey there," Amy said when she answered.

"It fits perfectly," Kat said.

"Great! I can't wait to see it!" she cried.

Kat had lost several pounds in her trance; she was extremely thin. She had placed eating on the back burner during her escapades trailing Ryan and Sophia. Amy had mentioned on numerous occasions that Kat was getting too thin, and it frustrated Kat at times. Amy had no idea what Kat had been dealing with.

"I have a few last-minute things to grab for the ball. How's your day look?" Kat asked.

"I have a meeting this morning, but then I'm free. You want to meet up for lunch?" she asked.

Spotting Amy leaving Sophia's apartment building still lingered in Kat's mind. "I'd love to. How about Benji's Bar? Outdoor patio?"

"Sounds great. I should be done by noon. See you then."

Kat didn't wait long to be seated. She'd arrived before Amy. She debated her approach. How would she ask Amy about being in NoHo without implicating herself? Amy would, in turn, ask what Kat had been doing there, so she needed to be prepared.

Amy rushed in. "I'm sorry. My meeting ran longer than expected. Jules is on one—imagine that," she said as she rolled her eyes.

Jules was the publisher's HBIC over the business and advertising department. She and Amy had a history of clashing.

"How is Jules?" Kat laughed. She knew Amy was not a fan of Jules. Kat always had liked Jules. Of course, she'd had a great rapport with the entire staff before she was dismissed. After Noah had passed, many of her colleagues had reached out to Kat, but she'd neglected to respond.

"She's still a bitch. She won't be remembered as the woman who kept her mouth shut—that's for sure," Amy replied.

Kat wanted to laugh. *A little hypocritical coming from Amy,* she thought. She let it go. "All ready for the party tomorrow, I assume?" Kat asked.

"Yes! I'm all set. My friend Celia is coming to do my makeup. She has partnered up with some photographer from California who relocated here recently. Anyway, she's coming over tomorrow. I can ask her to do yours as well."

"Oh no, thank you. I think I will do my own. I appreciate it, though," Kat responded. "Did you ever find heels?"

"I did. They are unbearably uncomfortable, but they look amazing! I'm sure they will come off at some point before the evening ends." Amy laughed. "Did you?"

"Actually, I did. I went down to NoHo the other day to do some shopping and found the perfect pair," she said slyly. She had not found her shoes in NoHo and had no idea about the shopping in that area. "In fact, I saw you that day! I meant to mention it last night, and it totally slipped my mind."

"Speaking of last night, well, that was awkward. A new job and you tell no one? What's up with you? Also, my God, Baron. Is he single?" she asked.

"I was planning on telling you and Ryan that evening. I seriously had no time to tell anyone. The day was a blur; it all happened so fast. It wasn't a secret. I had only sent my résumé the day before and had no idea they would hire me on the spot," Kat replied.

"So is he single?" Amy asked.

Of course she isn't really interested in my new job, only the hot man I'll soon be working with. "I have no clue. I met him that day, and I'm sorry I failed to ask any personal questions upon my interview." Kat laughed. "Besides, what about Tom?"

"Tom who?" Amy giggled.

"So anyway, I found the perfect pair, and mine are comfortable and sensible for a long evening," she said mockingly.

"Well, great. You were always practical and sensible before—" Amy stopped. "I'm sorry. I didn't mean—"

"No, it's fine, Amy. I know. Thank you for being a great friend. I needed someone to tell me to get my shit together. I fell apart. The world moved on, and I stayed behind. I'm just taking it one day at a time." Amy was fidgeting, and Kat could tell she felt remorseful about her comment. "Really, Amy, everything is fine. Let's have a nice lunch! It's a beautiful day, and we have an exciting event to look forward to. Let's order a drink."

They ordered two skinny margaritas, and Amy relaxed.

"So Monday, huh?" Amy smiled at Kat.

"Yep, I'm really looking forward to working again," Kat replied.

"Shit, yes, with that gorgeous Spanish senor, I would be too! How old do you think he is anyway?" Amy asked.

Kat felt silly that this man intimidated her. "I really don't know. Maybe fifty-five?"

"He's what they call a silver fox. I bet he knows how to properly handle a woman." Amy giggled.

Kat needed the conversation to change direction; she was flustered. "OK, OK, Amy, calm down. First line of business Monday morning: interrogation of Baron Marco." She laughed.

"I would appreciate that, and thank you." Amy swigged down the last of her margarita.

"Would you ladies like to order an appetizer or another margarita?" the waitress asked.

Amy answered, "One more for me, please. Kat?" Amy scrunched her nose and looked at Kat.

"Oh no, thank you. I'm good. I will have the ginger pork lettuce wraps, please," Kat told the waitress.

"Is that it?" the waitress said.

"That's it. Thank you," Amy responded.

"OK, so NoHo. What were you doing there?" Kat asked once again.

Amy looked up at her. "I wasn't in NoHo."

Kat was taken aback. "I saw you on—"

Amy interrupted her. "I haven't been to NoHo in some time. Maybe it looked like me. My doppelgänger." She laughed.

"Well, I guess so," Kat said.

The rest of the lunch was awkward. Amy finished her second margarita and claimed to have to get back to the office. She blamed it on Jules. She hugged Kat and rushed off.

Why would she lie to me about being in NoHo? Kat was certain it had been Amy, or at least she thought so.

Kat returned home and made sure she had everything ready for the next evening. She decided to get her office ready at home again, as before, she often had brought work home with her. She wanted to be prepared for the new job. Ryan had left a note saying he would be home late, and of course, she wondered why. She rang his cell.

"Hello?" he answered.

"Hey, how's your day been?" she asked.

"Same as usual. I finalized the deal with the intrepid client I mentioned before."

"That's great news," she said eagerly.

"Yes, finally. It's definitely a relief. I left you a note. Did you get it?" he asked.

"Yeah, I was just making sure I didn't need to have dinner ready for you. I mean, I can have something ready to warm if you'd like," she replied.

"No, that's not necessary. I can find something here at the office. Thank you, though. I'll see you later tonight. I love you."

"I love you too," she said.

It wasn't unusual for Ryan to work late. She knew that, but given the circumstances, she was suspicious. After the recent weekend they had spent with each other, she'd assumed they'd rekindled their love. She had been a fool. She'd believed he would break it off with Sophia and come running back into her arms. She still was hopeful that would be the case. Was he meeting Sophia that night? She had half a mind to find out.

She ran a bath. She loved bubble baths. They relaxed her— usually. She felt uneasy; the suspense was wrecking her. She hopped out of her bath and dressed. She hailed a cab and headed to Manhattan.

She arrived. It was dark, and the building was lit up. Maybe Ryan had been telling the truth; maybe they were still working. She checked her phone: 10:12 p.m. She couldn't very well walk in at 10:12 in her sweat suit; it would have embarrassed Ryan. The car was home, as it was often faster in the mornings to take the subway, which he had clearly done, so how was she to know if he was in there? She could call the office, she thought, but she knew they transferred the phones at six o'clock, so no one would answer. She couldn't sit out there and wait for him to walk out; he would potentially beat her home or, worse, see her. *This wasn't very well thought out*, she thought, scolding herself.

Just as she walked toward the subway, she saw Amy walk out of his building. *What the fuck?* she thought. She lost it. She screamed, "Amy!" *No more naive optimism.* She crossed the street frantically. A taxicab blew its horn at her, but Kat didn't care. She continued crossing, unaffected by the attack of the horn sounding.

"Kat, my God, what are you doing? You almost got run over! Jesus Christ." Amy stared at her.

"What are you doing leaving Ryan's building at ten o'clock at night?" Kat shouted.

"Calm down. I've never seen you like this. Are you OK?" Amy asked.

"Answer the damn question, Amy. What are you doing here?"

Amy looked worried. "I had a late meeting with Ted Thompson. Apparently, they finalized a deal with Intrepid, and we are doing a piece on it. Shelly's grandfather passed away this afternoon, and she couldn't make it. We couldn't risk losing the piece to another paper. Ryan did me a favor and convinced Ted to meet with me. What is going on, Kat?"

Kat was humiliated, standing there in her sweatpants, confronting Amy, now speechless. "Don't tell Ryan I was here," Kat begged.

"Why are you here, Kat? What is going on?"

"Nothing. I wasn't feeling well—that's all. I saw you, and I don't know what happened. I'm so sorry. I have no idea why I yelled at you." Kat began sobbing.

Amy was shaken. "Kat, let's get you home."

TWELVE

Kat awoke the next morning with Ryan lying beside her. She didn't remember getting home. All the stress had apparently really gotten to her. She did remember screaming at Amy. She sat up and felt faint and drained. She made it to the restroom and washed her face. She looked at herself in the mirror; she had bags under her eyes. *Great,* she thought. *Of all days.* She searched the bathroom cabinet for Advil and swallowed down two pills. She gathered herself and headed to the kitchen to make coffee. Ryan was still asleep in bed. He had taken the day off for the charity event and was planning to get a haircut. The party started at five, and Tom and Amy were coming over early to ride along in a limo Ryan had arranged.

Kat sat for coffee on the rooftop, rehashing the shit show she'd created the night before. She'd attacked and insulted Amy and basically accused her of having an affair with Ryan. It was Sophia she wanted to attack, but instead, Amy had taken the blitz. She felt terrible about it, and she wondered if she should call Amy. But what would she have said? She had already apologized for it. *"Oh hey, Amy, my husband has been having an affair for months now, so excuse my meltdown last night."* Yeah, *better not.* She would deal with it that evening—or not. Amy would forgive her; she would attribute it to her losing Noah and consider it a lapse in judgment. She was safe. Amy always seemed to understand Kat's meltdowns since Noah; she was patient and devoted.

Kat's phone buzzed, and she checked the time: 8:08. It was an unknown number. "Hello?" Kat answered.

"Good morning. Katherine Letty?"

"This is she."

"Yes, hello. This is Edward Shein with the *Manhattan Press*. We recently received your résumé and are interested in discussing this further with you."

"Wow, I feel so grateful for this offer; however, I have accepted another offer. Just yesterday, actually," Kat replied, trying to contain her excitement at another job offer.

"That's unfortunate. If you decide to reconsider, give me a call."

"Thank you for your consideration, and if this other falls through, I would love to follow up on this. Again, thank you so much!"

He hung up.

Two offers in two days! She concluded she evidently did not give herself enough credit.

"Good morning," Ryan said as he moved toward her on the rooftop. He had a cup of coffee in his hand.

"Good morning," she replied.

"Big night ahead of us. You prepared?" he asked.

She knew what he meant. She didn't acknowledge his question; she instead wondered if he had talked to Amy. *Did she tell him?*

"How do you feel this morning?" he asked her.

"I feel fine. Why do you ask?" she responded. She was a little hostile with her reply.

"I'm just asking, Kat. It's a big night is all. Lots of people will be in attendance. Just making sure you are ready for it."

"I'm getting pretty good at pretending everything is all right. I'll be fine. Thank you." She got up and walked downstairs, leaving him there shocked at her comment.

He left the house without telling her goodbye. Kat assumed he left for his haircut. She didn't make assumptions; she didn't care today. She was exhausted already, and her day had barely begun. She needed to get out of that house. She threw on some tights and her tennis shoes and decided to go for a run. Maybe exercise would give her energy. The city always helped too. She used to run every morning. She'd forgotten how much she enjoyed running and taking in the city's ruckus. It appeared busy to others but not to her; to her, it was alive.

On the way home, she stopped in a quaint breakfast nook. She had never noticed the place before. *A raspberry scone*, she decided. As she stood in line and finished ordering, she heard someone behind her say, "Make that two, please."

She turned. "Baron. Now I'm beginning to think you are following me," she said as she laughed.

Why was she so excited and giddy to have run into him? She felt little butterflies in her stomach. He had such a strong presence, almost demanding the room.

"Good morning, Katherine," he said alluringly.

She suddenly felt self-conscious as she looked down at her clothing. "I went for a run," she blurted out. She looked a mess. Sweat soaked her shirt. *Gray was a bad choice*, she thought, and she wore no makeup and had her hair carelessly tied back.

"Is the universe trying to tell us something, Katherine?" he asked.

"I'm sorry—what?" she replied.

"We keep running into each other. Is it fate or just coincidence? I'm teasing you. Let me buy you a scone," he said.

She was not offended but nervous. He made her nervous and sent her emotions into overdrive, as if she were a teenage girl.

"Sure, I'd love that. Thank you." She ignored all wisdom and common sense and sat down with him. She knew better. He was handsome and enticing. She felt guilty for a moment but then remembered how many times she'd watched Ryan and Sophia walk out of the hotel together.

"You live around here?" she asked.

"Not too far. I stop here a lot on my way to work. They have superb breakfast pastries, and I know the owner. She's an old friend of my family's," he answered.

"Well, I'm certainly glad I stopped in then. I love pastries, especially after a long run." She laughed.

They chatted for more than an hour. He was indeed single, Amy would be glad to know. He was divorced, with two sons. Most of his family were all back home in Barcelona, and some had migrated to France. He was interesting. He spoke Spanish, French, and English. He had grown up in Barcelona and moved to New York when he was twenty-nine. He was soft-spoken and not pushy but curious. He asked Kat a lot about herself and listened meticulously and intensely. It had been a long time since she'd really felt heard. She knew she had better go. She was not in a good headspace right now, and she was feeling vulnerable. She would definitely have let him take her to the bathroom and seduce her. *Who am I?* she asked herself.

"I am really looking forward to getting to know you more, Katherine. You're very lovely. I have really enjoyed this morning. You don't seem like a New York gal—that's for sure," he said.

"No? What is that supposed to mean?" She snickered softly and timidly pushed her hair behind her ears.

"Well, to be quite honest, you are so friendly, warm, and relaxed. Are you sure you belong in the city?" he asked as he laughed.

Kat found it ironic that he called her relaxed. She was not relaxed; in fact, she was the opposite at the moment. She was hiding it well, apparently, or maybe he had a way with her. She wasn't sure.

"Thank you for the scone and the company, but I probably need to head home," she said, and he stood with her. *Such a gentleman*, she thought.

"No, it was my pleasure. I am looking forward to Monday," he said.

She arrived home to shower and get ready for the ball that evening. Ryan had not made it home yet. *Who knows where he really is anymore?* she thought. She took her time in primping, thinking of her breakfast with Baron. She also thought of Amy. It was odd she hadn't called Kat to check in on her, especially after last night's charade. *It's fine*, she thought. She had intended on right-clicking her anyway. She was fearful of more questions or possible conflict after how she had behaved. It was bad enough they were going to the ball with her and Tom.

Ryan arrived home at three thirty. He had obviously been to the gym and had gotten a haircut. "Hey." He hovered in the bathroom.

"Hey," she replied.

"What time will Amy and Tom be here?"

"I haven't spoken to Amy today, so I'm not certain."

"The limo will be here at four fifteen to pick us up. Please let Amy know," he said. "You look pretty, Kat," he added.

"Thank you. I'm just about ready. Why don't you put on your tux and pour us a glass of wine before we head out?"

"Sure," he replied, and he left the bathroom.

She was relieved Amy had not called him about the night before. Kat sent a text to Amy: "Ryan said limo here at 4:15. See you soon."

Amy replied, "OK, thanks."

Amy and Tom arrived at four and joined Ryan and Kat in the kitchen. Ryan poured Tom a glass of wine.

"Ryan, I'm sure Amy would love a glass of wine; don't be rude," Kat said.

Amy quickly replied, "I'm good. Thank you." She looked at Ryan. "Kat, you look gorgeous, as always," Amy added as she fumbled through her purse for her lipstick. "Please excuse me while I use the little girls' room." Amy walked away.

Kat followed. "Amy, I'm sorry about last night. I don't know what I was thinking. I drank too much, and well, I was having a moment. Please forgive me. I really don't want this to be uncomfortable," Kat pleaded.

Amy dismissed Kat's apology, never acknowledging it. Kat followed her into the bathroom, where Amy began to primp in the mirror. They could hear Tom laughing in the kitchen. His laugh was obnoxious. He was obnoxious.

Amy rolled her eyes. "I don't even like him." She arrogantly laughed. "His laugh is hideous, isn't it?"

Kat started giggling. "Agreed. It's awful." She grabbed Amy's arm, and they left the bathroom.

THIRTEEN

The charity event was exquisite. There were rows of tables with elegant, detailed place settings and table centerpieces made with glass and floating votives. Each table had its own chandelier hanging from above. White linen draped the tables, and lines of roses in fancy vases surrounded the outskirts of the room. Kat felt out of place and insecure as she hugged and greeted several attendees. She had chosen a red Valentino gown with spaghetti straps, a plunging V neck, and a pleated flared skirt. She'd had it altered around the waist, and now she felt as if she were going to suffocate. Ryan was mingling, leaving Kat to fend for herself. She knew it was business. He had to socialize; it was part of his job and status.

She searched for Sophia. Was she attending? She walked around aimlessly, saying hello here and there, always secretly seeking Sophia. She ultimately made her way to the bar. She had lost Amy almost immediately after entering. Amy and Tom had had an argument in the limo and headed toward the restrooms—to argue some more, Kat figured. The place was packed with the most dreadful dresses and getups she had ever seen. She snickered to herself. She couldn't wait to hear Amy's insults later about the "costumes."

Someone touched her shoulder. It was Jules. "Hello, Kat. How are you?" Jules said as she reached in for a hug.

"Jules! Wow, you look amazing, per usual." Kat returned the hug. "I'm good. Better. Thank you."

"Listen, I'm really sorry about what you have been through. I tried calling you several times. I really wasn't sure what I was going to say, but I just wanted you to know I was thinking of you," she said genuinely.

"Thank you, and I'm sorry for disappearing on everyone. I wasn't ready to face reality. I had to come to terms with the fact that I will never get over losing Noah, but I can learn to live with it. And I am, day by day. Thank you again for your thoughts and calls."

Just then, Amy reappeared. "Hello, Jules. Fancy seeing you here," she said snarkily.

Jules hugged Kat once more and wished her the best before walking away.

"I'll order some drinks. What would you like?" Kat asked Amy.

"You know, Kat, I'm not feeling all that well this evening. I may call an Uber and head home," she replied.

"Head home?" Kat asked, concerned. "You feel that terrible?"

"Yeah. Tom is a dick, I don't feel good, and my shoes are killing my feet. I need to get out of here. You stay and enjoy your evening." She headed toward the exit.

Kat was baffled. This was way out of character for Amy. She was usually the life of the party, the first one to arrive and the last one to leave. Kat watched her walk away, still confused. She did not appear sick.

Amy made her way to Ryan, they conversed briefly, and then she disappeared. Kat was already feeling skeptical of Amy.

She wondered if she should call her to ask what was up. She didn't. She was more focused on Sophia's attendance or arrival.

However, there was still no sign of Sophia. Kat felt slightly relieved. She wasn't sure she was able to handle that pressure this evening. She had multiple conversations with strangers asking her how she was, and she gave the same response to all: she was doing well but had taken some time off, blah, blah, blah. She was like a record on repeat. Ryan occasionally made his way to her, stroking her on her back like a child. He was trying to be supportive; she knew that. They eventually made their way to the table, where Amy's seat was empty. Tom had stayed and thoroughly enjoyed the complimentary drinks from the bar, which amplified his unpleasant cackle. Kat wished he would have left as well.

The meal was amazing, just as she remembered from previous years. The starter included wood-oven-roasted tiger prawns and island creek oysters and was followed by an entrée of grilled Chilean sea bass with black truffle risotto. The dessert was a phenomenal chocolate Nutella soufflé that made Kat's mouth water. They shared a table with an investment banker named Todd and his wife, Martha, who were surprisingly down-to-earth people. Kat enjoyed chatting with Martha, and Ryan knew Todd, although she wasn't sure how. The evening persisted—still no Sophia. She evidently was not attending. Kat wondered why.

After dinner, Kat excused herself to the lavatory.

"Let me get that door, Mrs. Letty," she heard.

It was Martin Merrill, Kat's new supervisor.

She paused. "Call me Katherine. Nice to see you again, Mr. Merrill."

"Nice to see you as well, Katherine. I saw you in passing earlier, but I was tied up, and you vanished before I was able to say hello. The *Daily* has a table on the east end, doing our part for the children."

The Children's Scholarship Fund was hosted every year in New York City to provide tuition assistance to help low-income families send their children to college. Kat was proud of Ryan for participating in and contributing to the foundation. She had done her research before attending the first event previously. She was glad to know the *Daily* was a patron and contributor as well.

"I'm delighted to hear that; my husband, Ryan, and I have been fortunate enough to be part of such an impactful organization," she said.

He opened the ladies' room door for Kat. "Would love for you to meet a few more of your new colleagues later, if you'd like to join us for a drink on the east end." He laughed.

She smiled and accepted. "Of course, I would love that. Thank you."

She immediately regretted accepting the invitation. Was Baron attending? She had not seen him there. The thought of seeing him there made her nervous. Would she blush? Could she hide her schoolgirl crush? There were so many people gathered it was possible he was indeed there. *OK, Kat, get out of this bathroom.* She had hidden in the stall for as long as she could. Several ladies had come and gone. *Just say hello, and don't make eye contact with him.* She prepped herself. She felt silly again. Why did he have this effect on her? She saddled up, reapplied her lipstick, and walked out.

Ryan had made his way to another table, and she paused to watch him. He was good at entertaining, so personable. It came naturally to him; he fit in everywhere he went. She liked that about him, and she envied him. She made her way to him and grabbed his hand as she approached.

"Kat, dear, this is Peter Scott, an attorney with Hall and Associates. Peter, this is my wife, Katherine."

Shit, she thought. She couldn't speak; she was caught off guard. Peter worked at the same firm with Sophia. She began looking for her. *She must be here.*

"Kat?" Ryan said hastily to get her attention.

"Peter, yes, apologies. Nice to meet you," Kat said, never making eye contact with Peter.

"Wow, Ryan, you failed to mention how gorgeous your wife was. Nice to meet you, Katherine," Peter said.

Kat nervously smiled at Peter.

"She cleans up nicely." Ryan laughed. "I consider myself lucky."

Kat was still sidetracked. Where was she? Another gentleman approached and shook Ryan's hand, and they began chitchatting.

Kat stood there with Peter while Ryan continued talking with the other associate. Ryan excused himself to attend the bar with the gentleman.

"Did Miss Sophia Gantz not make it this evening?" she asked Peter. It was obvious Peter had been overserved that evening. He had slurred his words when he proclaimed how gorgeous she was previously.

"Well, considering she hasn't made it to work this week, I am guessing no. I haven't seen her," he replied.

"Hasn't made it to work this week?" she repeated.

Peter walked away toward the bar. He brushed up against a blonde in a dress Kat considered to be too short for such an event. *She didn't make it to work this week?* She was puzzled. She wondered why. She walked away toward Mr. Merrill's table.

There was no sign of Baron at the table. She was relieved yet disappointed. She wanted to redeem herself after the sweat-fest scene from the morning. She made her way around the table, and Martin introduced her to the rest of her future coworkers. Small talk about the charity and her upcoming role ensued, and she felt welcomed.

Her phone buzzed in her clutch with a text message from Ryan: "Where are you?"

"East table with the *Daily*. Are you ready to go home?" she answered.

"Yes, front in ten."

She said her goodbyes to the table and thanked Mr. Merrill once again for the opportunity and for the introduction. He was a nice man. He was very matter-of-fact, but she didn't mind that. She headed to the front exit. Just as she made her way out, she spotted Ted Thompson. He was head of marketing and sales at TAK Pharmaceuticals and one of Ryan's associates. She strode on over. "Hello, Ted. Nice to see you. It has been a long time. How are you? Are you keeping Ryan in line?" she asked as she quietly laughed.

"Keep Ryan in line? That's impossible." He laughed too. "How are you, Katherine?"

"I'm doing quite well. Thank you for asking. Congratulations on the Intrepid deal. That's wonderful news and, I'm sure, a big relief for all of you."

"Absolutely a relief. Thank you."

"I hear you met my friend Amy Harris the other night. I'm betting you were not able to get a word in." She laughed.

"Amy Harris?" he asked.

"For the piece on Intrepid," she said.

"I'm sorry, but I'm lost, Kat," he said as he picked up a purse from the table. "I apologize, but I must run. Claire has had a little too much vodka this evening, and I think it's best I get her home. She's in the car, waiting; she forgot her purse. Tell Ryan good night for me." He walked away.

She stood there in disbelief. *Amy lied to me again?*

The limo was waiting out front for her when she arrived. Ryan was already sitting inside, on his phone. By that time, it was eleven thirty. She opened the door.

"I was just about to text you," Ryan said as he turned his phone off.

"Yeah, I'm sorry. I ran into Ted Thompson on my way out," she replied, glaring at him. She waited for some sort or reaction. Nothing. He rested his head on the headrest and closed his eyes in the limo as they headed home.

An hour later, Kat lay in bed next to Ryan as he slept. He had gone to asleep almost immediately after arriving home. Kat couldn't sleep. Why would Amy have lied to her? Why had she been at Ryan's building that night? Amy was her closest friend. She told Kat everything—sometimes more than she wanted to know. Kat didn't understand. She rolled over to grab her phone and sent Amy a text: "How are you feeling?" Amy had now lied straight to her face twice.

CHAPTER

FOURTEEN

The next morning came. Kat checked her phone: 7:42 a.m. No calls or texts had come in from Amy. Ryan was still asleep in bed. Kat snuck out to make coffee on the roof. She reflected on the night before. She wondered why Sophia had not made it to work all week. She decided Ryan had finally ended things for good, and she must have been home heartbroken. *Did Amy suspect Ryan of being unfaithful and start investigating herself?* Kat asked herself. Why would she not have come to Kat? Did she think Kat couldn't handle it? Kat was puzzled. Did she know about Sophia? Was she surveilling her too? Kat was sure Amy had an explanation for her lies. Kat felt humiliated for all but accusing Amy of seeing her husband that night.

"Good morning," Ryan said as he arrived on the rooftop with his coffee.

Kat stood up and kissed Ryan. "Good morning. How are you feeling?" she asked as she smiled as she persevered through her uncertainties.

"Rested. I needed that. It's been a rough last few weeks, and last night felt like work," he replied. He sat with her on the couch. He gently rubbed her knee as he covered them with a blanket. "Can we sit here all day?" he asked.

She laughed. "I wouldn't mind that at all," she said. She was still somewhat relieved that Sophia never had shown. Maybe that meant he really had ended things for good.

"Are you excited about your first day?" he asked.

"I am. I want to feel like myself again. I miss working and feeling productive," she answered.

Kat never heard from Amy that day.

Ryan and Kat shared an uneventful day, getting ready for the next week. They grilled on the rooftop and had a few cocktails. Kat enjoyed the occasion, released all her insecurities, and lived in the moment. They caught up once again, making up for lost time, she supposed.

They never spoke of Amy or her bizarre exit the night before. Kat had her new job on her mind. She was excited and anxious, ready to rejoin civilization and feel productive. She couldn't help but think about Baron and wonder why he hadn't been in attendance last night.

Monday morning arrived. Kat stopped into the small bakery where she had run into Baron before, secretly hoping to run into him. He wasn't there; she saw no sign of him. She could have missed him, she thought. She ordered another raspberry scone and a coffee. Baron had been right; the scones and coffee were both incredible. She could see why this was a routine stop for Baron.

She made it to the *Daily* with twenty minutes to spare, and the receptionist greeted her once again.

"Good morning, Mrs. Letty. I'll show you to your office," she said.

Kat was a bit insecure, coming in as the new girl. Developing a new routine would be challenging, especially with the headspace she'd had over the last few months. She remained confident that she was capable, however.

The receptionist's tone was much different this time, gracious and friendly.

"I'm sorry. I'm not certain we have been formally introduced," Kat said.

"Yes, of course. Call me Libby," she responded with a laugh. "If there is anything I can help you find, let me know. I'm always around. My extension is 112. Mr. Merrill will be here in about thirty or so minutes. On Monday mornings, they always meet in the conference room to discuss the upcoming week."

Libby was an older woman and well kept. She reminded Kat of a woman straight out of the 1950s—vintage. She wore an A-line dress with a cardigan sweater. She had the brightest shade of red lipstick, which was perfectly in line with her lips, with no smudges at all. Libby appeared interesting, to say the least.

"Thank you, Libby," Kat said.

She familiarized herself with her new office and waited about fifteen minutes before making her way to the conference room. Her office was small but large enough to have two chairs and a minisofa to accommodate visitors or clients. The walls were gray, draped with framed *Daily* articles that held significance, articles they were proud of. In the conference room, there were four others gathered around the rectangular table upon her arrival. She had met most at the fundraiser. There was no sign of Baron.

"Good morning," she said as she took a seat.

All were hospitable and sociable. Small talk around the table continued. As she sat, her phone vibrated with a text from Ryan that read, "Good luck today."

Just then, Mr. Merrill walked in. "Good morning, everyone." He spoke as he took the head of the table. "Most of you have met Katherine Letty. We are proud to have her joining us as executive editor. Baron has had some unexpected family issues he's dealing with at the moment and will not be joining us today. So let's get on with it. Katherine, please listen in, and I will have Nora get you up to speed on some projects we will be discussing."

The meeting lasted about two hours. There was back and forth chatter around the table as she listened in. She sat quietly pondering what family issues Baron was dealing with.

After the meeting, Nora followed Kat to her new office, and they discussed in further detail the projects she would be handling. Nora left her with several manila folders filled with information to look over. Libby dropped in multiple times to ask Kat if she needed anything. Kat thought it was a thoughtful gesture. She felt guilty about her first impression of Libby the day she'd interviewed with Martin. She had thought of her as cold, but she was quite the opposite.

Kat didn't take a lunch break. She had her head buried in the information Nora had left with her. Libby came in to sit at about one thirty.

"Are you not going to eat, Mrs. Letty? I can run and grab you something if you'd like," she said.

"Oh, that is awfully considerate of you, but I'm good. I'm not hungry. First-day jitters, I guess. Thank you, though," Kat said.

"Nora can be cranky at times. Don't let her get to you," Libby said.

Nora was the creative director and came across as the no-bullshit type.

"Really, thank you, Libby. I'm good. It will just take me some time to sort through the material is all," Kat replied.

The day flew by. Kat did not get much accomplished, or at least she felt as if she didn't. Martin came by at about six o'clock and said, "Kat, go home. You can't do it all in one day."

He laughed. "See you tomorrow." He walked away toward the lobby.

Kat packed up her folders, grabbed her purse, and agreed to call it a day. She made her way out of the office and down to the subway station. She caught herself wondering what was going on with Baron. Just then, her phone vibrated with a text from Amy: "I'm sorry about this weekend. I didn't feel well, but I'm finally better. How was the first day?"

Kat replied, "Long but great. Just now heading home. Going to take me a minute to get back on track. Loved the crew. And glad you're feeling better."

Kat finally made it home. She had beaten Ryan home. Her cell rang. "Hello?"

"Hey, Kat, how was your first day?" Ryan asked.

"Well, it went well. I actually just walked in the door. Are you headed home?"

"No, I haven't left the office. I'm finishing up some things now, but I thought you may want to meet for drinks. Meet me halfway?"

"Well, I guess so. It would be nice to grab dinner. I don't feel like making dinner, honestly. That sounds fabulous. Where?"

"Quarter Lounge? They have some greats appetizers."

"Sounds great. I'll head that way. See you soon."

Kat was feeling more confident about her situation with Ryan. She presumed Sophia's absence from work could only mean one thing: he had ended things. She felt such relief that things were finally beginning to look up—well, minus her newfound fascination with Baron. The instant connection she'd felt with him could have been her vulnerability. Her life had been in such disarray for so long that she found comfort in him for some reason. He felt genuine and sincere. She was searching for stability, it seemed. Ryan had not given her that lately.

75

She made it to the Quarter Lounge, paid the cab driver, and headed inside. She sent Ryan a text on the way inside: "Are you here?" The bar was small; she could scan the whole place—no Ryan. She took her coat off and sat at the bar.

"What can I get you?" the bartender asked as she placed a napkin in front of Kat.

"Dry martini, please. No olives. Thank you," she answered.

It was a charming place. Kat had never been there. It was posh. She wondered if Ryan had been. He evidently had, as he'd acknowledged the great appetizers. She received a text from Ryan: "Running late. See you soon."

Great, she thought. *A thirty-minute cab ride to sit alone for God knows how long.* She scanned her emails while she waited.

An hour passed. Kat was frustrated. She sent another text to Ryan: "Should I order us an appetizer? What do you recommend?" No answer.

She was becoming impatient, working on her third martini. Just as she stood to head to the ladies' room, the large flat-screen hovering above the bar caught her eye. A picture of Sophia appeared on the screen. *What the fuck?* Below her photo, text read, "Missing: Sophia Gantz." Kat froze in her tracks. *Missing?* She was stunned, in disbelief. She felt a surge of gut-wrenching pain, as if someone had hit her in the stomach with a bat. She rubbed her eyes, making sure her eyes weren't playing tricks on her. What the hell was going on?

She couldn't hear. The music drowned out the TV. She sat back down, grabbed her phone, and began searching the internet for information. She was so flustered she could barely type out Sophia's name.

She clicked on an article and read, "Sophia Gantz, a twenty-eight-year-old woman, was last seen on August 17 by her colleagues at Hall and Associates in Manhattan, New York."

She couldn't read any more. She felt sick. Did Ryan know she was missing?

Her phone buzzed with a text: "Almost there." It was from Ryan.

Shit. She ran to the ladies' room and locked the stall. "I'm in restroom. Sitting at end of bar. Be out shortly," she wrote back.

She was panic-stricken and felt as if she were going to pass out. *Did he have something to do with this? I mean, she suddenly disappears after he, I'm assuming, breaks her heart? Was she so heartbroken that she is hiding away? Did she refuse to end it, and they had a huge altercation?* Her mind was running away. *He absolutely could not,* she told herself. She was sure this was all a misunderstanding.

She walked out of the restroom and headed toward Ryan. "Hey," she said.

He kissed her cheek and took a seat next to her. "I'm sorry. Ted called a last-minute meeting just as I was about to leave. How was your first day? Tell me all about it!" he said excitedly.

She sat there unable to speak; she was still in shock.

"Kat, are you all right?" he asked.

"Ryan, I don't feel well. I had three martinis, and well, I must go home now. I'm not well. I'm sorry. We need to go." She stood and grabbed her coat and purse.

"Kat, wait. I mean, have you paid?" he asked.

"No, I haven't," she said as she headed toward the door. She waited for him in front of the bar, wondering what the fuck to do. What could she do? He didn't even know she knew about his affair with Sophia. Just then, he walked out and grabbed her hand.

"I meant to tell you the drinks are stout here." He laughed.

She felt like screaming, "I'm not drunk, you asshole! Your

fucking mistress is missing!" But she remained silent, using her martinis as her scapegoat.

Kat closed her eyes on the way home and didn't speak a word. Ryan made small talk with the cab driver. When they arrived home, Kat rushed into the house and went straight to the bathroom, locking the door behind her.

Ryan knocked on the door. "Kat, can I get you anything?" he asked from behind the door.

"No, thank you. I am sorry. I just feel like I'm going to be sick," she replied.

After upchucking three martinis, she made her way to the kitchen to grab a glass of water. Ryan was sitting at the kitchen table with a bowl of fruit.

"You feel better?" he asked.

"A little," she answered while gulping down the glass of water.

"I was looking forward to hearing about your first day," he said, extending the bowl of fruit toward her.

"No, thank you. I'd better not. Those martinis did not agree with me. I should stick to chardonnay, it seems. The day went well. Naturally, I was flooded with lots of information in one day."

"Of course," he said as he leaned back in his chair while looking at Kat.

"I think I should lie down." She took a deep breath and headed toward the bedroom.

Kat lay there in bed, contemplating confronting Ryan. *For once in your life, Kat, don't stay silent. Shout it from your lips. Ask him. Challenge him*, she told herself.

Ryan came to bed about an hour later. He tucked in close to her, wrapping an arm around her waist and pulling her in. His skin felt cold. His hands slid between her thighs, and his forearms brushed against her. She felt afraid of him in that moment but wasn't sure why. He felt like a stranger.

Kat awoke early, before Ryan, leaving him asleep in bed. She needed to run. She needed to relieve some frustration. Her mouth felt dry, and her stomach hurt. It was stress and anxiety. Where was Sophia? A run would help settle her before work. She threw on her tights and a T-shirt and took off.

So much had happened in a month. She considered that maybe she was losing her shit again. Was this all an illusion? Had she slipped into some schizophrenic episode unknowingly? Was she in a coma? She could only hope. Anything was better than her reality at this point, she thought. Amy, Sophia, Ryan, Baron—it was all too much. Or she had made it easy for everyone to deliberately lie and cheat on her. She was overcome with fury; sweat had already saturated her hair and her shirt. She felt her heart beating in her throat, and she curled her fists involuntarily. She stopped. *I am weak*, she told herself. *Not because of Noah. I've always been pathetic.* She hated herself in that instant. It was comical to her to think she had made a comeback. The truth was, she didn't like who she was, pitiful and powerless. This was who she had always been. This was where it had taken her. She walked the rest of the way home.

Ryan was leaving as she approached the door. He was dressed for work, carrying his briefcase. "I tried calling you to see where you were, but your phone rang from the bathroom," he said.

"Yeah, I left it here. I went for a run." She kept walking as he stood there watching her walk away toward the entrance to their apartment.

"Well, I guess I will see you tonight then, Kat. Have a great second day," he said as she walked on in without saying a word.

CHAPTER
FIFTEEN

Kat made it to work early. Libby, at her desk, greeted her with her glasses perched on the end of her nose. "Good morning, Mrs. Letty—I mean Kat," Libby said as she looked up at her and smiled. "May I bring you some coffee?"

"Actually, that sounds great, Libby. Thank you," Kat responded, and she continued toward her new office. She wondered if Baron was going to be present that day. Libby had given her a tour of the office the day before, and Kat had noted Baron's office was on the way to the restrooms. She placed her purse and coat on her desk and made her way to the restroom, secretly snooping on Baron's office to see if he was there. The light was off; again, there was no sign of him. She was disappointed, although she didn't understand why—she didn't know him well. She thought perhaps she was subconsciously diverting from reality and the problems she was facing: her cheating husband, her lying best friend, and the missing mistress.

Libby set her coffee on her desk. "Here you go, dear. Two sugars in case you need them."

"Thank you. Is Mr. Marco in today?" she asked Libby. "I had a few questions for him."

"Oh no, he isn't. Apparently, his niece is missing," she said quietly as she looked around Kat's office apprehensively. "No one has heard from her in quite some time. It's been all over the news. I'm betting Nora can help you if you need something."

"His niece is missing?" Kat said. Her eyes widened.

"Terrible." Libby shook her head, fretting. "Apparently, the family is in shock. No one has been able to contact her. She just seemed to vanish into thin air. I've heard the whispers in the office. It doesn't sound good."

"That is terrible." Kat felt a rush of blood to her cheeks. "His niece—she is from here? Lives here?"

"Yes, she is an attorney for a huge law firm here in Manhattan. A beautiful young lady. Apparently, she was doing some online dating. I pray nothing has happened to her. That online dating is dangerous. I don't understand all that. We didn't do that in my time," Libby said.

Kat felt goose bumps overtaking her body, and her throat felt as if it were swelling and blocking her air. "I'm so sorry to hear this. I will keep Baron and his niece in my thoughts. Thank you for the coffee. I should get started on these files."

Libby closed the door on her way out.

Jesus Christ. Sophia was Baron's niece. Kat grabbed her trash can and threw up. She then thumbed through the files piled on her desk, unable to make sense of any of it. Her mind was overtaken by Sophia, Ryan, and Baron. Had something happened to Sophia? She had not disappeared; people didn't disappear, at least not for no reason. Had she been online dating and seeing Ryan? Kat wondered if Ryan knew yet. Would he be distraught? Would he confide in Kat? She couldn't think straight. She grabbed her purse and her coat and walked out of her office.

"Libby, I will be back. I'm following up on something in a file. Be back later."

"Yes, ma'am," Libby replied as she gave her a thumbs-up and answered the phone.

Kat hailed a cab and jumped in. "Take me to 101 East Forty-Second Street, please." Kat headed to Amy's office. She needed someone to talk to.

She sent Amy a text: "I'm headed your way. It's important."

She paid for her cab and headed inside the office. *Amy must be in a meeting.* She would wait. She'd received no text back from Amy, but she proceeded inside anyway. She slung open the door to the office and marched through.

"Hello, Kat."

She heard a familiar voice, but failing to look back, she kept moving. She scanned the lobby while making her way to Amy's office, seeing several familiar faces but neglecting to return any greetings. Amy's office door was closed, with the lights off.

"Kat, you OK?"

She turned around to see Jules staring at her. "Is Amy here?" she cried out.

"No, she isn't. Come to my office, Kat. Sit down with me, please. You don't look well," Jules replied.

Kat nodded and followed Jules without saying hello to anyone. Everyone looked at Kat with a blank stare, gawking. It felt like a nightmare she'd had in high school—as if she were walking in on the first day of school and looking down to see herself naked. Awkward.

Kat sat down on a couch in Jules's office.

Jules sat next to her, looking at her oddly. "Kat, you look upset. Are you OK?"

"I just need to talk to Amy. Where is she?" Kat asked, agitated.

"Is this about Ryan?" Jules looked down as she asked.

"What? What do you mean? What about Ryan?"

Jules touched Kat's knee and looked her straight in the eye, saying nothing.

"Jules, what do you mean?" Kat asked again, feeling guarded.

"I'm sorry. I thought you knew. You came in here like a tornado. I just figured." She stopped.

"Knew what? Figured what? What the fuck are you talking about, Jules?" Kat asked, lifting her voice. Kat began to breath heavily, and she had another urge to vomit. She cupped her mouth and gagged.

Jules stood and grabbed a trash can and a tissue.

"Where is Amy, and what the hell are you talking about? Please, Jules, just say it. Everyone is gawking at me out there because I disappeared. Because I'm a crazy person because I lost my son." She flailed her arms in the air. "I'm not crazy. I needed some time. That's it. I'm fine. I just needed to talk to Amy is all. I've had an insane day and—"

Jules interrupted her. "No one thinks you're crazy, Kat. I'm sorry about your day, and until the charity event the other evening, I had no idea you and Amy were still friends," Jules said intensely.

"Why wouldn't we be?" Kat asked.

Silence filled the room. Jules bit her bottom lip and turned her head from side to side, looking around the room. Kat knew her well enough from working with her to know that she did this when she felt uneasy.

"Listen, Kat, Amy and Ryan—" Jules paused.

"Amy and Ryan what?" Kat shrugged, confused.

"They were having an affair, Kat." Jules took her hand off Kat's knee and grabbed her hand. "I'm sorry. I thought you had found out. She never mentions you anymore, and well, then you come storming in here. I was confused the other evening at the ball, and well, I don't know how much more I should say here."

Kat began to sob hard. "No, no, you have it all wrong. She spent time at the house for me. She had dinner with him. I mean, she helped us through losing Noah. It's a misunderstanding." Kat wiped her nose and eyes with the tissue. Her words were shaky, and she was trembling.

Jules began wiping the mascara from Kat's face. "Kat, I think we need to get out of here. Let me take you to my apartment."

Kat nodded and left with Jules.

CHAPTER
SIXTEEN

Kat didn't return home that evening. After Jules's house and her recent revelation, she could not face him. She had been reckless to put so much trust into one person, let alone two, uncritically. Such acceptance of his behavior was unacceptable, a far cry from loving someone unconditionally. She had let passion and love overwhelm her judgment. She never had taken reasonable precautions to avoid being victimized. It was partly her fault; she had let her compulsion of avoiding the risks of losing Ryan and of having confrontations cloud actuality. She'd fabricated the man she expected him to be. In the beginning, she'd established who he was and put that ideal safely into a box, never to reexamine it. They had initially constructed what she'd thought to be an accommodating, devoted relationship, and it had been at first. So she'd held on to that.

Her hotel was cold and dark, as was her life in that instant. Her phone rang over and over. Ryan was attempting to get a hold of her. He sent her texts repeatedly: "Where are you? Are you OK? Call me. Kat, please. What's going on?"

Amy finally responded to Kat's previous text, apologizing for being out of the office, and tried calling Kat five times and sending basically the same texts as Ryan: "Are you OK?" Why did Amy care? She had betrayed Kat unforgivingly.

Kat concluded there was a critical distinction between blame and responsibility where she was included, but it did not justify what they had done. Kat might have been able to forgive Ryan for his situation with Sophia but not with Amy; that was not the same. She felt humiliated once again. She thought about all the times Amy had lain in her bed with her, consoling her, pretending to be loyal. All the while, Ryan had claimed Amy irritated him, and maybe eventually, she had. Kat didn't care. It was irrelevant.

She had thanked Jules for being honest. She never had given her the opportunity to before. Kat had avoided the outside world for almost a year. Jules had told her that after Kat lost Noah, she could not be responsible at that time for any more heartbreak, and Jules had said she would not have had the nerve to tell her anyway, considering all the despair Kat had already encountered. Jules had spared her the details, never revealing when the affair had begun or how long it had lasted. It didn't matter; the damage was done.

Kat had a hard time understanding Amy's motivation for helping her heal; after all, Amy was the one who'd encouraged her to get her shit together. Kat presumed Amy needed her healthy so Ryan could move on to her. Did Amy know about Sophia too? Kat wasn't sure. Jules was unsure if Amy and Ryan were still seeing each other. It didn't make a difference to Kat. She was dazed, to say the least. She powered off her phone and shut her eyes. Her last reflection was on Baron. She wondered how he was doing.

Kat managed to make it to work the next morning in the clothes from the same day. She never went home. No one at the office seemed to notice, and if they did, they did not make mention of it. After a phony good morning to Libby, she headed to her office. She did not look well; she was even paler than usual, and she had not eaten the day before. She still felt sick to her stomach. Still undecided about her plan and where the fuck she was going to go, she managed to start skimming through her files.

Baron peeped into her doorway and said, "Hello, Katherine."

She raised her head in surprise and looked at him. "Baron, good morning."

"May I come in?" he asked.

"Absolutely," she replied.

He sat in the chair in front of her desk, and she began awkwardly moving things around on her desk, not sure what to say to him.

"How's the new job treating you?" he asked while he interlocked his hands together and sat up in his chair.

She had an overpowering urge to get up and run. Did he know about Ryan and Sophia? She remained in her chair calmly, although she felt a sudden burst of sweat roll from underneath her breasts. Her head began to throb, and a shaky gasp escaped her. "Well, it's going well. Thanks for asking." She felt her chest rising and falling rapidly. She briefly explored the random thought of a legal obligation to spill her guts and expose what she knew. She wasn't ready to have that conversation, she concluded. She was already stressed to max capacity.

"How are you doing?" she said genuinely with a hint of sadness in her eyes.

"You've heard. We are devastated, confused, and frustrated. It's not like my niece Sophia. She's a good girl. The police have had no luck in locating her, although they have some leads they are looking into. We are just praying she's OK."

"You all have been on my mind." She wasn't sure how to answer, given the circumstances.

"I could really use a drink after work, and it looks like you may need one as well. Would you like to join me? That is, if you're able?" he asked.

She hesitated.

Libby came across her office phone to announce she had a call on line two. "It's your husband, Mrs. Letty. I'm sorry. Kat."

"Can you please tell him I am in a meeting and will call him shortly?"

"I sure can. Thank you." Libby hung up, but she called back a moment later. "Kat, he says it's urgent."

"Not now, please, Libby!" Kat said.

Baron sat across from her with a peculiar look. "Everything OK?" he asked uncomfortably.

"Yes, I will take you up on that drink, Baron. Thank you."

"OK then." He stood and moved toward the door. "Let me know when you finish up later, and a drink we shall have."

Baron was enjoyable. He was genuinely nice, or so it appeared. He was an older, mature type. He moved slowly and spoke softly, and he was assured but not cocky. Libby had declared he was the office catch but not interested in the dating scene. Libby knew the office tea and had shared some about him in their banter back and forth over the last few days.

Kat walked to the lobby. "I'm sorry if I sounded a little unpleasant, Libby. It was not intended toward you. I ask that you deflect any calls from my husband for me today, OK?"

"Trouble in paradise?" Libby winked at Kat.

Kat just smiled and winked back, trying not to strain the situation further.

Kat returned to her office and struggled to complete some projects. She finally powered her cell back on, and multiple text messages from both Ryan and Amy relentlessly came through. She did not read any of them.

She read one from Jules: "Hope you got some rest. I am here if you need me."

Kat determined that Amy hated Jules because Jules knew about Amy and Ryan. Amy wanted Kat to detest her as well, fearing she would divulge the truth to Kat. It made sense now. Amy had been visiting Ryan on the evening when Kat caught her leaving his office so late. The audacity she had and the unnecessary guilt Kat had placed on herself for accusing Amy of such! *Bitch.* It was a word Kat never used, but today she did.

Baron showed up at Kat's door once again. "It's almost six. Are you about done?"

"I am. Let me grab my purse and use the ladies' room, and I'll meet you in the lobby."

Kat hurried to the ladies' room and made a half-assed attempt to look presentable. She once again had skipped lunch, and she was starving; she felt weak. *This will have to do,* she thought.

She looked down at her cell phone on the bathroom counter as it vibrated with a text from Ryan: "I'm almost to your work. I need to know what's going on with you. You can't just not come home. Are you all right?"

Funny he should fucking say that, she thought. He hadn't come home a few weeks ago, and she knew he hadn't been at the cemetery all night.

He'd sent the message at 5:56 p.m., which meant she had just enough time to leave before he arrived. The last thing she needed was an embarrassing quarrel in front of Baron.

"I'm ready; let's go." Kat rushed into the lobby.

"I've got a place in mind. I'll get us an Uber," Baron said as he looked at his phone.

"Can we walk? I need to get out of here. Long day." She smirked at him.

"Sounds good to me." They headed out.

CHAPTER
SEVENTEEN

Their destination was a restaurant, not a bar, and Kat was appreciative. She was in no mood for a bar, and she was certain Baron was not either. The place was quiet, with dim lighting. They had walked for a bit but ended up catching the subway. The ride had been quiet. He seemed a bit gloomy, but so was she. When they sat, he pulled her chair out for her. *A polite act*, she thought. It almost seemed like a date, but Kat didn't go there. She had more to worry about. She was just grateful they had missed Ryan. With her phone powered back off, she relaxed and ordered dinner and a glass of chardonnay.

"Your niece Sophia—do they have any idea where she has gone? I really hate that you and your family are going through this," Kat said.

"To be honest, Kat, I'm unsure she went anywhere. I really believe the police think something has happened to her. Not sure if someone harmed her on her way home or kidnapped her or if someone she was seeing could have been involved. Sophia was a beautiful girl, Kat. To my knowledge, she was seeing or chatting with several men. They are trying to get phone records now; everything is a process. Her phone and laptop haven't been located. You wouldn't believe the amount of missing-person cases in this city. It's truly upsetting."

Kat didn't know what to say. She wanted to let slip "Yes, my husband was one of the several," but instead, she remained quiet, only nodding in shock while sipping her wine. She would have hated to implicate Ryan for no good reason. After all, Kat had just about convinced herself Ryan had nothing to do with Sophia's vanishing, so what would have been the purpose in mentioning it?

Baron had ordered an old-fashioned, a concoction of bourbon and bitters with a tinge of sugar. That was fitting, she thought, as he seemed to be the old-fashioned type, still pulling out the seat for a lady and opening doors. Chivalry was not dead, she thought.

Focus, she told herself, although it did feel good to have the distraction of his physical features overpowering her.

"Would you excuse me? I need to use the ladies' room," she said as she stood.

Baron stood with her as she excused herself. "Of course. May I order you another glass of chardonnay while you're gone?"

"That would be great."

She headed toward the restroom, pilfering through her purse for her lipstick. Her phone was still powered off, and she reluctantly powered it on. An overwhelming number of messages from Amy and Ryan began invading the screen. They were basically still the same: "Please call. Where are you?"

She decided to send him a text: "I am fine. Need some space. Will talk soon." There was much more she wanted to say, but she needed to find the courage and collect herself. By now, she was certain that Amy had heard Kat had come to her office and talked with Jules and that the cat was out of the bag. She was sure Amy had told Ryan, and they were scheming up a bullshit story to tell her. As if it weren't enough that his current mistress was missing. That was Kat's life: always taking a backseat and going with the flow and never stepping on toes or speaking out of turn. She was at her breaking point, and she felt it. Maybe she would fuck Baron for revenge. It was tempting. She immediately powered her cell back off.

She returned to the table, where her glass of chardonnay was waiting for her. Baron was away from the table. He reappeared shortly with his phone in hand. He sat down, appearing flustered, as he placed his phone on the table.

"Is everything OK?" Kat asked.

"Apologies, Katherine. That was my sister. Apparently, she just spoke with the detective on Sophia's case. No news. She is frustrated. This has been so tough on my family. Not knowing if she is alive or what has happened to her. They want answers." He paused. "I don't want to go home tonight." He stared at her with a lost look.

The truth was, Kat didn't either. She was as lost as Baron was. Sleeping with him that night was clearly off the table. That would have been taking advantage of him, she thought. They were both vulnerable and broken.

"Well then, where to now?" she replied as she hesitantly smiled. She reached across the table and took his hand. She meant for it to be a friendly gesture. "Baron, I am so sorry. I don't really have any words to relieve you. I wish I did. I know this is so difficult for you and your family." She felt guilty. She knew her husband was seeing Sophia, and she wanted badly to tell him.

He examined his hand in hers and looked up at her.

She pulled away. "I'm sorry. I wasn't—"

He interrupted her. "No, Katherine, it felt good. I'm very drawn to you." His eyes widened as he reached over and took her hand in his. "I know you're married." Shame filled his face, but he didn't let go of her hand, and she didn't let go either.

"Can we go?" she asked.

He stood, walked over to her chair, and helped her up, saying nothing. He ushered her out of the restaurant in silence.

"Listen, Baron, things are complicated. I mean at home." She glanced up at him.

They began to walk down the street with no place in mind.

"Same," he said with a light laugh. "You make me crazy, Katherine. Since the moment I met you, I can't seem to get you off my mind," he added, echoing exactly what she was thinking. He stopped and gazed at her, threading his fingers through her hair and tucking it behind her ear. "I have never crossed any lines with a married woman or even entertained it, but the lines are blurry, Katherine. I'm having trouble with the lines. So please tell me to go home. Tell me you're not interested."

Her voice cracked. "I can't tell you that I'm not attracted to you; I would be lying. It's just—well, like I said, things are complicated." She pulled away and began walking as he followed. "My husband is having an affair," she blurted out. "With my best friend. Well, they were. I just found out. It's such a long story. You don't want to hear all this. I'm damaged, Baron. You don't know me."

He grabbed her by the waist, spinning her around to meet him face-to-face. "I want to know you." His face was beautiful; his eyes were innocent. "Everyone is damaged, Katherine. I'm damaged. We just all wear our scars differently."

The intensity in his voice was real. He was damaged too, she realized in that moment. He hid it well, unlike Kat. He had scars, just as Kat did.

Sophia crossed her mind. What about Sophia? "There's something else, Baron."

With admission on the tip of her tongue, he jilted forward, kissing her. The kiss snowballed out of control. He pushed her against the street wall as she kissed him back, igniting a desire like no other. There was a desperation in his touch and in hers as their bodies mingled. She finally pulled away.

"I can't. We shouldn't." Her hands were shaking, and her body was still pulsating. People walked by as if nothing were happening.

"OK. You're right. I'm sorry, Katherine. Let me walk you home."

"No, thank you. I mean, I am not going home. I'm staying in a hotel," she said.

He stood there pleading with his eyes.

She wanted to say yes; she yearned for more. "Thank you for dinner, Baron, and the company. I think it's best we say good night. I am not sure if I could resist taking you up to my room. I am married. You and I work together." She knew there was more. *My husband was having an affair with your missing niece.* "But I will see you at work tomorrow." She stood on her tiptoes and gently kissed his cheek and then began walking in the other direction.

She reached the corner and hailed a cab. "Take me to 45 West Forty-Fourth Street, please."

She revisited the fiery kiss on her ride back to her hotel. The evening had unquestionably escalated. She thought about Ryan. She felt zero guilt. Was this a new Kat? How had she gotten Ryan so wrong? How had she not suspected him and Amy? She concluded she had really checked out, but even so, it didn't merit his sleeping with her best friend or Sophia.

EIGHTEEN

Kat slept better than she had in years. She wasn't certain if she was that exhausted or content. Baron had a hold on her, a spell. Although they'd shared only a kiss, it had been satisfying, uplifting, and motivating. She decided she would meet Ryan after work to address the Amy situation. Ryan was no longer her safe place, and on the horizon, she envisioned her future self. Her grandfather had once told her to stop looking for happiness in the same place she had lost it. She pulled out her phone and turned it on. She sent him a message: "I'll be home after work. Please don't call me." She jumped onto the subway and headed to the *Daily* to work.

"Good morning, Libby," she said with a smile as she entered the lobby.

"Well, good morning to you, Kat," Libby said, lifting her coffee cup to her as if giving a toast.

Kat rounded the corner and headed toward Baron's office. Peeking her head in, she saw he was sitting in front of his computer.

He removed his glasses when he saw her. "Hello, Katherine." He started to stand.

"Don't get up. I just wanted to say good morning is all." She gave him a smirk and headed to her office.

Kat worked through lunch. She was determined to get some work accomplished. As she sat in front of her computer, her phone hummed with a text from Jules: "You OK? I've called a few times."

Kat picked up her phone and rang Jules.

"Kat, I'm glad you called. I was worried."

"Hi, Jules. No need to worry. I'm good. I really am. I should have called. I've had my phone off, avoiding Ryan and Amy."

"Yeah, about that. Amy knows you came by looking for her. She hasn't spoken a word to me. I'm assuming someone told her you were in my office and left upset. Not that I am concerned about her feelings."

"I'm sorry about that. I guess I did cause a small scene." Kat laughed lightly. "You know, I take that back: I'm not sorry." She laughed fully this time. "Thank you again, Jules. Those things aren't easy to disclose to someone on the edge of a nervous breakdown." Again, she snickered.

"You sound solid, Kat—different."

"As painful as this all is, I've been through worse. That being said, I plan on meeting Ryan at the house tonight."

"Well, please call me and let me know if you need anything."

"Thank you, Jules. I don't plan on disappearing again. Something tells me I will be OK. I refuse to be stuck where I don't belong. Talk soon."

As she hung up her phone, she felt energized. She believed the words she had to said to Jules—she would be OK. As for Amy, she decided she would also handle her. Kat couldn't believe the audacity she had in coming into her home and pretending to be loyal. That was for another day.

She didn't run into Baron that day. She stayed in her office working, making calls and looking over a stack of files. She left the office at five thirty, heading home. Ryan had abided and had not attempted to call her, but he had returned the text: "OK, please come home and just talk to me."

She took her time in heading home. Scenarios raced through her mind. Would he be honest? What would his reaction to her newfound courage be? She never had crossed him. She never had felt the need to. She felt blindsided. Had she brought this on herself? *No, Kat, don't try to justify his decisions.* She felt as if she had swallowed a painkiller. The pain was absent; she felt fury. She pictured them in her home, in her bed. She revisited the moments of watching him and Sophia leave the hotel together. It was provoking her wrath. *You've got this, Kat.*

She entered the building and headed up slowly with patience. As she approached the door, she paused to take in a deep breath.

As she turned the knob, Ryan appeared. He leaned in toward her and wrapped his arms around her. "Kat! Jesus, what is going on?" he sputtered.

"You tell me, Ryan." She pulled away from his arms and headed toward the kitchen.

He followed hurriedly. They stood in the kitchen. He didn't dare move toward her; he only observed from across the kitchen, puzzled at her behavior. His eyes were filled with tears, though they did not fall from his eyes.

"I have been worried to death, Kat. This is not like you."

She crossed her arms her against her chest. She felt tense, her mouth felt dry, and she had an urge to jolt, but she remained in place.

He stared at her, waiting for her to say something. "Say something, please," he begged.

Her throat was parched as she tried to swallow. "I said you tell me what's going on. What has been going on?" She turned and sat at the table. She gazed at the vase on the table, and then she calmly picked it up and launched it across the room, shattering it against the wall.

"Jesus Christ" was all he said. His eyes were fixed on the shattered glass.

Kat continued to sit in the chair, not cracking under pressure. "Let's keep this, Ryan. Tell me about how you fucked my best friend while I mourned the loss of our son."

Ryan's legs nearly gave way. She looked as he regained his balance and approached the table to sit. Beads of sweat were evident across his forehead. A rush of nerves flowed through his veins as he took a seat. His heart was pounding. He said nothing for several beats.

Kat's teeth were clenched as she anticipated his reaction, his answer.

"Kat, it happened once. It meant nothing. I was lonely."

"Don't you dare. Do not try to justify this. I was lonely. I was mourning!" she shouted.

"It meant nothing. I love you. I had a weak moment. Please. I was lost too. You aren't the only one who lost a son, Kat."

"Really? I did not run out and lie down with a stranger! I did not commit adultery!" She continued to scream.

He sat at the table with his head in his hands, unsure how to respond. She was right, and he knew there was no appropriate answer or comment. He began to sob.

Kat felt a sense of calm overtake her. She paused before continuing. "Ryan, I have been a good wife. I have always been sensible and considerate, being careful not to be too overly sensitive or speak out of turn. I admit I took longer than I should have to heal. I neglected you. But I never betrayed you. As I fought to reclaim myself, alone, you were deceiving me.

No offense, but fuck you. I did not deserve this. And we both know there is more."

He continued to sob silently. Tears submerged his red face. Kat rose from the chair and filled herself a glass of water. She felt no remorse for her strike. *Cheating is a choice, not a mistake,* she reminded herself.

Ryan removed his hands from his face and looked up at Kat. "I messed up, Kat. I'm sorry. I know I have made mistakes, but I never meant to hurt you." His voice quivered.

"There was undeniable distance between us when Noah died. I'm not disputing that. I just can't excuse your conduct because of it. You lied and cheated—multiple times, Ryan, not just once. This was not an accident; these were choices you made over and over. I lost my self-respect at one point, and I am ashamed of myself for allowing this, for watching this unfold. I did, Ryan—I watched all of this unfold. I didn't have the courage to confront you. Now, Amy was a surprise, I must admit—the icing on the cake."

He knew she knew about Sophia, although he was unable to summon the nerve to say it. She could see it in his eyes. His eyes appeared unfeeling to her; he was lost in thought. He was replaying multiple occasions in his head of his and Sophia's dealings, pondering the extent of what she knew. He was careful not to incriminate himself, cautiously choosing his next sentence.

"I am not debating about the choices I made. I fucked up. I know this," he said meticulously, not mentioning further mishaps. He was no longer sobbing; he was shocked. He was shocked Kat knew what she knew. He had been coasting on cruise control, never noticing her, he realized. She had emerged from her stupor, catching on to his exploits.

The room was filled with silence, along with uneasiness,

as both deliberated how the hell this had all happened. Before Noah had died, they had been inseparable, hopeless romantics prioritizing each other, or at least that was what they both had believed to be true. They had both dreamed of a family, kids running around, Sunday afternoons in the park, ice cream, and birthday parties. All had shattered with Noah's passing; the future had become nonexistent after he died. They both had been unsure what the future held for them without him. It was as if Ryan and Kat had never existed before him; they had forgotten who they were. There was no one to blame for his death; they both understood that, but the wreckage to follow was another story, at least in Kat's mind.

"Where is she, Ryan?" she asked sternly.

"I haven't talked to her. She sent me a message saying you came to her office upset. That is all. I haven't spoken to her, and I don't want to speak to her, Kat. I don't care if I ever see her again."

"No, Ryan. Where is Sophia?" she said.

He looked stunned. His face became white, and he immediately squirmed in his chair. "What do you mean?"

"What do you mean what do I mean? She's missing. Where is she? Her family is looking for her. The police are looking for her." Kat's face was agitated, and she was angered and irritated. She thought of Baron and the family's anticipation of her return.

"I don't know," he replied, dramatically pressing his forehead against the table and placing his hands in his lap. He stayed that way, not moving a muscle.

"Ryan, she's missing!" she shouted as she grabbed his shoulder, pushing him up.

His face was still white, and his voice trailed off. "I said I don't know. I can't do this right now. I'm sorry. Please, can we lie down for a bit? Please."

"You can't do this right now? You're sorry? What are you sorry for? That she is missing? That you were having multiple affairs? You must be joking, right? Lie down with you, Ryan? Don't insult me. I'm done lying down with you."

Ryan stood and shouted at Kat, "I am not solely responsible for all of this, Katherine! You checked out of our marriage as well. No, you did not sleep with another man, but nonetheless, you deserted me! I lost Noah too, and you left me alone to grieve! You persistently pushed me and everyone else away. This is significantly more deep-seated than an affair. I needed companionship. I was walking alone in grief. This was not vindictive; I did not do this to hurt you. This was not a reflection of how I feel or felt about you. This was me needing someone— anyone—to fill a void! So stop standing there without blame; you are no better than me. I will not sit here and listen to you demean me and my choices. I will not argue that what I did was right. I am a reasonable man, but I did what I had to do at the time. I slept with Amy once, and it meant nothing. I had an affair that went on too long with Sophia. I broke it off. Kat, when you came alive again, I came alive again. It was all I wanted. I wanted you back, Kat. That weekend we spent together inspired me. I am sorry for what I have done. I broke it off with Sophia. Kat, I don't know where she is. That is the truth."

Kat stood in front of Ryan, face-to-face, stunned and speechless. Had she convinced herself that he was to blame for everything? Had she let her anger and emotions fog her clarity? A sudden feeling of apprehension consumed her mind and body. She needed to lie down; she felt faint. *Typical, Kat. Always second-guessing yourself.*

She made her way to their bedroom and, with shoes and all, sprang herself onto the bed to close her eyes. Ryan soon followed. She felt him cautiously sneak into bed, careful not to touch or stir her.

Morning came with the sun penetrating through her eyelids. She looked over to see Ryan asleep beside her, and the sight of him next to her made her stomach turn. She fumbled out of bed and downstairs to search for her phone. It was 8:48 a.m. She had several missed calls that morning from an unfamiliar number, with a voice mail notification. That would have to wait, she thought. She needed to gather some things without waking Ryan and get out. She made her way upstairs to her closet. She took a bag for her toiletries and some clothes for now. Ryan was sleeping hard. *Rough night*, she thought as she rolled her eyes and crept by with her bag in hand. She walked out the door with nowhere to go. Normally, her first choice would have been Amy's, but clearly, that was not an option. Her phone rang again. This time, she answered. "Hello?"

"Katherine."

"Baron, hello."

"Listen, I know it's early and Saturday morning. I hope I didn't wake you, but we haven't discussed the other evening, and I really wanted to apologize."

"No, you didn't wake me. I'm actually on my way out. I don't need an apology, Baron. I kissed you back, remember?"

"Do I remember?" He laughed. "I, in fact, do remember. I can't stop thinking about it. I have replayed that moment in my head more than a dozen times."

"Listen, it's really not a good time, Baron, so—"

He interrupted her. "Please come by. Let me make this right and apologize. I promise to keep my lips to myself. I feel an apology is necessary. I was way out of line. You're right. You're married."

Kat had nowhere to go and agreed. She was aimlessly

wandering the city, attempting to make a plan about where to go from there. Baron convinced her to visit him. He sent her his address, and she surrendered, making her way to his apartment.

When she arrived, he was waiting in the lobby. "Nice place," she said as she gawked at the artsy displays overcoming the lobby.

"Thank you. It's comfortable. Come up. We can have a cup of coffee." He started walking toward the elevator.

Kat was holding her bag.

"Let me take that for you. Are you heading somewhere?" he asked as he took the bag from her hands.

"Well, not really. I mean, yes, but I'm not certain where yet. I left Ryan this morning," she said as she draped her head in the elevator. A single tear ran down her cheek.

"Katherine, I am so sorry. I know this is difficult." He wiped the tear from her cheek. "Nowhere to go? Katherine, stay here." He held up his hands as if in defense. "I won't pressure you. I won't cross any more lines. If you have family or friends you can stay with and don't feel comfortable staying here, I would be glad to take you somewhere."

"I have a friend I could stay with—Jules. I just don't want to burden anyone. She knows my situation—well, most of it anyway. We recently reunited, and well, I'm not certain I feel completely comfortable asking that of her quite yet."

"Stay with me, please. I have plenty of space. I will be a complete gentleman. Honest."

They walked into his apartment, which was spacious, tidy, and bare, much as she would have expected a man's residence to be. He had the necessities, Kat assumed. She saw no pictures hanging or large displays of family photos inhabiting the space. It suited him. The couch was leather, with one blanket hanging on the corner. Although bare, the place felt comfy. The lighting was magnificent; there were lots of windows. She was certain it was expensive to reside there; she knew the neighborhood, and it was not for the blue-collar laborers.

"Is your family not staying with you?" she asked him.

"They had to return home. They plan on returning with any news or findings, of course."

Just as they entered the kitchen, Kat's phone rang once again. It was the same number from that morning. "I'm sorry, Baron. Let me take this," she said as she excused herself to the living area.

"Hello?" she answered.

"Good morning, Mrs. Letty. This is Detective Ferguson with the NYPD," an unknown man's voice said. "I have been attempting to reach you for several days now. I have also left several voice mails."

"Yes, I'm sorry. I have had my phone powered off for the last few days. How can I help you?" she asked, confused.

"Can you come down to the station and meet me in person so we may chat?"

"On Saturday? I'm sorry, Detective, but I am a bit confused. How can I help you? What is this regarding?"

"Mrs. Letty, we would like to speak with you concerning Sophia Gantz. We understand you knew her."

Kat felt as if the blood were draining from her body; weakness hit her. She sat on the leather couch. It was cold, yet she began to feel sweat pool beneath her knees as she sat. Baron walked in with a cup of coffee in hand.

"Yes, I can. Give me an hour." She hung up.

"You OK?" Baron asked. She was pale. He handed her the coffee.

Kat immediately set the coffee down on the table in front of the couch. "I must run. Thank you for the coffee. I have to take care of something." She rose from the couch with weak knees, barely able to stand up straight. She was dreading speaking with the police, although in her gut, she had known this was eventually coming. She felt faint once again. "My bag—where is it?" she asked Baron as she shuffled toward the kitchen.

"Katherine, leave it. Come back. Let me take you where you need to go. You don't seem OK." He looked puzzled.

"No, no, thank you; I can get there. I'll leave my bag. Thank you, Baron. I just need to—I'll be back," she said as she made her way to the front door, escorting herself out.

She needed to get out of there. She was dodging any more questions he was bound to ask. She was unsure if she would return, but she was in a frenzy to get out of the apartment, terrified the detective might call her back. How would she explain that to Baron?

NINETEEN

Kat caught a cab to the nearest police station. She had hung up so abruptly she wasn't quite sure where to go. "I'm looking for Detective Ferguson," she told the officer manning the front desk.

"Take a seat, ma'am," the officer responded. "Is he expecting you, Miss …?"

"Mrs. Letty, and yes, he is," she answered. Kat was no longer wearing her ring. She had left it on the bathroom counter before sneaking out that morning. She was surprised Ryan was not blowing her phone up. She assumed he'd drunk too much the evening prior after their argument and was sleeping it off.

"Ma'am?" The officer peered back into the lobby at Kat. "Follow me, please."

She obliged and followed the officer into what appeared to be a bare room.

"Have a seat. Detective Ferguson will join you shortly." The officer left, shutting the door behind him.

She looked around and wondered if this was an interrogation room. It was small, with nothing hanging from the walls, only four chairs and a table and some stacks of papers sitting in the corner. Was she about to be interrogated? Did she need an attorney? She was nearing a full-blown panic attack. Her breathing was heavy and rapid. Just as she picked up her cell phone, a gentleman appeared at the door and walked in. He was older, heavyset, and balding. He came in bare-handed and greeted Kat with a "Thank you for coming."

"I am unsure why I am here," she said.

"I am Detective Ferguson with the NYPD. Nice to meet you." He reached out to shake her hand.

She reached her hand out to his but only glanced down at his hand and back to his round face. "Detective, excuse me for being short, but again, why am I here?"

He sat, unbothered by her gesture not to shake his hand. He appeared relaxed, leaning in on the table with his elbows and hands sitting on the tabletop, intersecting. "Sophia Gantz. That is why we are here. I'm sure you are aware that we have also sat down with your husband, Ryan."

"No, in fact, I was not aware!" she exclaimed. She wanted to scream. *No, he left out that he was questioned by the police about his missing mistress. He isn't sharing much these days; in fact, he also failed to tell me that he was sleeping with her in the first place. Oh, and my best friend. So no, he did not mention this to me.* She wondered if Ferguson had been informed that she knew about the affair. She was unsure. She sat there in silence, waiting for his response.

"Mrs. Letty, you do know your husband was having an affair with her, don't you?" He looked at Kat, waiting for her reaction.

"Do I need an attorney?"

"You tell me. Do you?"

"Are you implying that I had something to do with her disappearance?"

"I am not implying anything, Mrs. Letty. I am just trying to figure out what has happened to Miss Gantz. In a case like this, we investigate all avenues—jealous spouses, family, friends, coworkers. Your husband was seeing Miss Gantz. Were you aware?"

"I'm not having this conversation without an attorney present. I had nothing to do with her disappearance, and I pray you find her. I know nothing of her whereabouts or if something has happened to her. Now, if I may go." She stood from her chair.

"You certainly may go, Mrs. Letty, but don't go far."

She could not get out of that station fast enough. What the hell was happening? Was she a suspect? Did Ryan know? Clearly, Baron didn't know; he had just offered up his home to her.

No wonder they hadn't found Sophia; that detective was awful, she thought, approaching her and all but accusing her of Sophia's vanishing. *How could he suspect me?* she thought. *On the other hand, how could he not?* Ryan had made a mess of things.

She sent Ryan a text: "You failed to tell me the police questioned you about Sophia. Of course, that's your thing these days: keeping secrets. Now they are questioning me."

Kat felt she should clear the air with Baron. As humiliating and difficult as it would be, she knew it was the right thing to do. He had confided in her about Sophia, the family, and the pain they were all going through. She felt obligated to let him know the truth, particularly after he had reached out and extended her a place to stay through her tough time. She felt she had inadvertently lied to him by not offering up the truth. What had she planned to say the first time they'd spoken about it? *Oh yeah, actually, it's my husband. She was seeing my husband.* The night he'd kissed her and professed his interest in her, she'd had it on the tip of her tongue until the kiss derailed her. She should have told him that night. Her intentions had been good, but of course, being typical Kat, she had run.

⁂

Kat tapped gently on Baron's door, secretly hoping he wasn't there, so she'd have another opportunity to run and to avoid.

He opened the door. "Come in." He opened the door wider and gestured her inside. "I'll be honest: I wasn't sure you would be back. You seemed shaken earlier. Hope all is well."

As Kat entered his apartment slowly, she felt a tingling in her chest, a burning sensation, brought on by her nerves. The thought of confessing everything she knew rattled her to the core. Would he turn her away? Would he yell and scream or call her a liar? That would make for an interesting work environment for sure.

"May I have a glass of water?" she managed to ask. "I need to talk to you."

"Sure," he said with a concerned look on his face. "Let me grab you some water."

He left the living room and headed toward the kitchen. He returned with a glass of water, still looking somewhat anxious. He handed Kat the glass, and she swigged it down as if it were a last meal on death row.

She sat on the couch once again, staring at his face. He was stunning. He sat across from her with his hands on his knees.

"What is it, Katherine? Are you OK?"

She felt a tear run down her cheek and quickly wiped it away. She was certain her face had turned red, as she could feel the heat radiating off it. Focused now on holding back an ugly cry, she searched for her words. "I don't know how to say this,

110

Baron. I have been at the police station. That is where I hurried off to."

"Are you in some trouble? What's happened?"

"It was about Sophia." The moment she spoke, she felt as if a thousand cactus needles plunged into her body. It was painful.

He sat back in his chair, appearing baffled, as he ran his right hand through the front of his hair, seemingly thinking hard about what she had said. His hand made it to his lips, and he ran a finger over his bottom lip multiple times; it must have been a nervous gesture, she thought.

"Sophia? What do you mean? Did you know her? Do you know where she is?" he asked as he sat back up, leaning forward with his hands back on his knees, staring Kat right in the eye.

"Yes. I mean no. My husband knows her." She hung her head in shame, breaking the intense eye contact with him. She gazed at the floor, waiting for him to respond.

He quickly stood and began pacing the room, and the lines around his mouth seemed to deepen. "Do they work together? What do you mean they know each other?" he asked, still appearing puzzled.

"No, Baron, they do not work together. My husband, Ryan, was seeing Sophia. She was the one he was having an affair with," Kat stood in front of him now, looking straight up at him with apologetic eyes. "They had been seeing each other for a few months."

The puzzled look disappeared, his eyes widened, and his cheeks slightly flushed. He now seemed to be drifting in thought, unbothered by Kat's presence in the room.

"I am sorry. I should have told you. I was ashamed and embarrassed. I have no idea where she is. Ryan claims he doesn't either. Please say something." Kat gently touched his arm.

Baron looked down at her hand on his arm. He didn't move.

"Katherine, this is a lot of information for me to process right now. He doesn't know where she is? What did the police say?"

"They did not say much. They asked me questions. If I knew they were seeing each other. Told me not to go too far. Baron, I would never—I mean, I have no idea what has happened to her, if anything."

"Have the police questioned Ryan? I am assuming at this point they have." His voice had become louder, and every word was more intense than the last. He was fidgeting and seemed to be growing angry. His body became tense, and his face was now bloodred. She could see the veins on his temples pulsating.

"Yes. I did not know until Detective Ferguson told me today," Kat replied. She removed her hand from his arm and looked around the house. "I will grab my bag and go. I'm sorry, Baron. I really am."

Kat searched the house for her bag and found it sitting on a bed in what appeared to be the guest room. She promptly grabbed it and headed toward the apartment door. Baron was still in the living room, with his hands now resting on his hips, pacing.

"Katherine!" he called out. "Please stay. I am just shocked. I'm not angry with you; I am angry with the situation."

She loved the way her name rolled out of his mouth, and she loved that he was so proper in calling her Katherine. His accent made her name sound sexy. Even in this moment, she thought he was sexy.

She paused at the door; she had already reached out for the doorknob, which sat in her hand. She turned around and looked at him. He had moved closer to her and was gazing at her from across the room. He looked broken and sad. His veins were no longer pulsating.

"Please. I need you here. None of this is your fault. We

crossed paths for some reason, Katherine. I guess it was fate after all."

With some relief, she let go of the doorknob and walked toward him. He embraced her in his arms, holding her against his chest. She felt silent tears roll down her face as she pressed it into his body. They held on to each other for what felt like an eternity, saying nothing.

That evening, she stayed with Baron. They ordered dinner in and never spoke of Sophia or Ryan. It had been an exhausting day, and she wanted it to end.

As they sat across from each other in the living room, Kat caught Baron examining her intensely many times. "Why do you keep looking at me that way?" She smirked as she asked. "Do I look tired? Because I am." She laughed.

"I find you breathtaking is all. I find comfort in looking at you. I told you I would not do that, but I can't help myself. I should go to bed," he said.

"Thank you." She paused, looking down at her hands while fidgeting. "I guess it's obvious I feel the same."

"I'm glad you're here."

"I don't want to intrude, though. I'll figure out a more permanent place to stay as soon as I can."

"No rush. I'm enjoying your company. Stay as long as you'd like. I will, however, let you be before I misbehave once more." He cast her a side look while removing his blanket and standing from the couch. "Good night. Is there anything I may get you before I turn in? I gave you the tour; you know where the towels and things are. Anything else?"

"No, I'm good. Thank you, and good night to you," she said as she smiled at him.

She lay there on his couch. The apartment smelled of him. Her cell phone on the coffee table between the couches remained off. She opted to power it on. She had several voice mails from Ryan and one from Amy. She erased Amy's message—she was not willing to hear her out or deal with anything else at the moment. She listened to Ryan's messages, and they all sounded the same, pleading for her to call him. She didn't.

The television was playing an old mobster movie with Spanish captions below. She had not yet heard Baron speak Spanish; it was probably a good thing—it would have topped off the indisputable sex appeal he already exuded. She would have a hard time with boundaries and self-control, she realized.

After the movie, she made her way to the guest bedroom.

TWENTY

The next morning was Sunday. Kat slept surprisingly well in the foreign bed. She planned on doing some research on apartments for herself online and then contacting a Realtor at some point. She couldn't go home. Kat was conflicted, unable to truly come to terms with the situation. One part of her believed Ryan was not capable of hurting someone, but on the flip side, he had fooled her with the affair, lies, and manipulation. The man she initially had married never would have deceived her. He had changed. What else was he capable of? She reflected that morning on many memories of their marriage, good and bad. Although most were good, things had fallen apart, mostly after Noah. Ryan had resorted to being unfaithful and believed Kat was somehow responsible for it. She reassured herself he was no longer the Ryan she had married in the beginning. That morning, Kat took a little extra time in getting ready; she would be sharing space with Baron and did not want to disappoint him. She was thankful she and Baron had found each other. They needed each other; both were entrapped in terrible circumstances.

As she emerged from her room, she found Baron sitting

at the table, holding a cup of coffee. "Let me make you some coffee," he said as he rose from the chair to the Keurig.

"Thank you. Good morning." She took a seat at the table.

"It's a good morning now," he said as he brewed her coffee and glanced over his shoulder. "How did you rest?"

"Very well. The bed is pleasantly comfortable."

"Great. I'm sure you needed the rest. We both did after yesterday. Creamer?"

"No, black is fine. Thank you."

He reached over the table and handed her the coffee cup, sitting down next to her.

"I was going to explore apartments for rent in the area today. I will have to run home to grab my laptop at some point. I was in a hurry to leave, and well, I only grabbed some necessities."

"That's not necessary. Use mine. You're welcome to anything in this apartment." He grinned.

His grin stirred up arousal in her body. She almost felt powerless when he smirked or smiled. She felt her body stiffen. "Thank you. I think I should grab a few more things, though." It was an excuse, she supposed, to get out, because if she stayed in that apartment all day again with him, she was bound to give in to temptation.

"Then let me go with you. I don't think you should go alone, Katherine," he said firmly.

"I'm sure you have things to do. I don't want to burden you. I'll be fine. But thank you."

"I insist. There is no telling what that hombre is capable of." He paused and touched her hand. "I'm sorry. I should not have said that."

There it was. She found herself more focused on the way he rolled *hombre* off his tongue than the actual assertion itself.

"No apology necessary. I understand. I am not defending

him by any means, but I am certain he is not capable of hurting someone—well, in that manner, I mean. Although he isn't the man I married, he's never physically hurt me. I mean, he has changed indeed, but I don't think he will hurt me."

"People can surprise you, Katherine, and maybe people don't actually change; maybe you just never knew who they really were."

Kat felt reluctant to respond. She debated in her mind his argument. She sipped her coffee and gazed out the window.

As Baron disappeared off to his room, Kat grabbed her purse and jolted out the door. She knew he would continue to debate with her about visiting Ryan alone if she didn't make a run for it. She refused to be afraid of Ryan, although she did contemplate his involvement with Sophia's disappearance. He had never been physical toward her and never had appeared violent in any situation. She could do this.

She was out the door for six minutes before Baron called her. She right-clicked him and sent him a text: "I'll be fine. Be back soon. Don't let me invade your Sunday routine. Please."

As the cab pulled up, she deliberated about getting out. Her hesitation was due to her fear of confrontation; she wasn't feeling threatened. She knew this visit would devolve into more conflict and hostility in which they would reach no agreement. However, she needed her laptop and some other toiletries she had failed to grab yesterday morning. She was also going to tell Ryan she was moving out and finding her own place. Ryan had been her best friend for six years; it wasn't easy, even after the distress he had caused her and the sadness she endured from his choices. He had been the stability in her life, the only person she had truly confided in, the one person she had trusted. She didn't find pleasure in the pain this would cause him. *These are the consequences*, she decided. How could she ever trust him again? After all, he'd had multiple affairs, not a slip or a onetime blunder.

The door was open. She walked in to find him sitting at the table. He appeared unkempt and tired.

He stood when he saw her. "Kat." He was wearing sweatpants and an old T-shirt. Both were wrinkled, and she knew he had not changed his clothes since she'd left the previous day. His face was sunken and unshaved.

"I am only here to grab some more of my belongings. That's it," she said confidently.

"Can we at least talk for a moment? Please. Just sit down. I'll make you some coffee."

"No, I do not want coffee." She did sit down on the opposite end of the table.

His eyes followed her to her seat and remained on her while he also sat.

"I have plans to move out. I need some time to find a place. So I will keep the majority of my things here until I have that sorted out."

"Moving out? Kat, please. Don't do that. I told you it meant nothing. I need you. Please." He pleaded with her.

"I am not having this conversation again. I can't. I am tired and overwhelmed. I also know the police questioned you about Sophia. They questioned me as well."

He sat up straighter and pushed himself up higher in the chair. "God damn it, Kat, I don't know where Sophia is. I told you that. I told that detective that too." He was now glaring at her, and she could tell he was angry; the blood was pulsing in his neck veins. "I would never!" he shouted, and then he paused. "You know I am not responsible for her disappearance. She probably intended to cause a scene. I broke it off with her, and it made her extremely unhappy. She craves attention and is used to getting her way. I hope to hell she is OK, but I could not tell you where she is."

"The police told me not to go far. What on earth does that mean, Ryan? Do they think I'm some vengeful wife who murdered her husband's mistress? Somehow, I take the fall for this? This is insane. I don't even know what to make of it all."

"I doubt they think you have harmed her, Kat; they are doing their job. They said the same thing to me," he said quietly. He was now hanging his head, with his eyes fixed on the table.

"Before Amy and Sophia, did you ever cheat on me? Tell me the truth, Ryan. Was our whole marriage, my happiness, a facade?"

"No, I was faithful to you, Kat. I mean, before Noah. After Noah, I—" He stopped, shook his head, and then put his head in his hands. "I don't want us to end." He sighed.

"Neither did I. It's too late. You all but blamed me for your conduct. I am not responsible for the choices you made. You are; that is on you. It's hard for me to believe that you had anything to do with Sophia's disappearance, but I can't defend you either, as it seems I don't know who you are any longer. I will be moving out, as painful as it may be. We can iron out the details later. I don't have the energy right now, and it appears you don't either. You look terrible. Have you even eaten anything in the last two days?"

"I'm not hungry," he replied, still holding his head. He didn't look up.

Kat stood up and walked to the kitchen. She made her way to the pantry and grabbed some bread. "I'll make you some toast before I pack."

Ryan didn't move. He was as still as a deer in headlights; he looked frail and defeated. She recalled the last time she'd seen him that way, the day they'd buried Eve. Her gut felt twisted, and she felt a trace of sorrow for him. She placed a small plate of toast on the table and pushed it toward him.

"Just eat some toast, OK? You need to eat."

Kat departed from the kitchen and walked upstairs to their bedroom. The bed was still unmade, and the bathroom was untouched since her leaving. She knew he had not visited the bathroom. He never tidied up; Kat always did. After he used his toothbrush, it always remained beside the sink, and the hand towel remained next to it. He always left his bath towel on the floor. She noticed because she picked up after him daily as if he were a child. It used to irk Kat. She would ask him to tidy up after he showered, but he never did. He was relentlessly messy.

She packed up more of her things, this time grabbing a large suitcase. She heard him dragging his feet up the stairs and toward the bedroom. He stood there silently in the doorway of her closet and watched her pack.

"Did you eat your toast?" She looked up at him.

"No, I can't stomach anything right now. Thank you, though," he answered softly.

As she zipped her suitcase, she noticed the airline baggage tag still attached. It was from one of their last trips: Illinois. Ryan had persuaded Kat to visit Ottawa to get lost in nature with him. They had hiked the Starved Rock State Park trails. Although it had not been a traditional romantic getaway, they'd had a remarkable time. She clutched the tag and tugged, tearing it off.

Ryan staggered out of the doorway and plopped himself onto the bed. He lay there staring intently at the ceiling while she jostled the bag into the bedroom. She hovered above him, looking down on him. He continued to stare at the ceiling, never moving his eyes to hers.

"Clean yourself up, and eat something, Ryan, please."

He said nothing. She began to pull the bag out of the room. He sat up swiftly, blinking at Kat, who turned to look at him. "Kat, I regret this. I really do, and I am sorry."

Kat did not respond; she only darted out of the room and headed toward the front door.

TWENTY-ONE

Kat left her things in the extra bedroom Baron graciously supplied her. Her better judgment told her to stay elsewhere, but she opted to go against it. Baron was not home when Kat arrived, but he had left the door unlocked—she assumed for her. She was a bit relieved she could unpack without having to explain herself and her encounter earlier that day. After unpacking, she fell onto the bed. The room was small and clean but bare, like the rest of the house. It did have towels and such but felt cold, unlike her own bedroom. She wasn't really convinced the room was cold; she was just feeling lost, and after all, it was technically a bachelor pad. She reached out to Jules. Kat had several unreturned messages from her and decided to let Jules know what was happening.

"Hello, Kat. So glad you called. You OK?"

"I am. I'm sorry. I had to take care of some things, and I just feel, well, overwhelmed once again. I told Ryan today I did not plan on coming home."

"How did he take that news? Where are you staying?"

"Not so well. Of course, he's pleading for forgiveness. It's so complicated—all of it. Amy is only the tip of the iceberg."

"I'm sure he is. Do you need a place to stay? You are more

than welcome to stay with me. I mean, I haven't a lot of room in my studio, but we can definitely make it work."

"I am staying with a new friend from work. Thank you, though. I would like to have lunch and talk. There is just so much more to this story, unfortunately." She heard the front door open from her room. "Listen, Jules, let me know when we can get together. I just wanted to let you know I am OK, and thank you for everything. Talk soon." Kat hung up the phone and collected herself for the upcoming chat.

She poked her head out the door to see Baron standing in living room. He had gone for a run or exercise of some sort, it appeared. He was sweating and had jogging pants and a sweatshirt on. His hair was messy but in an almost delicate way. He was holding a bottle of Fiji water, chugging down the remainder.

"Hi." Kat apprehensively spoke from the doorway. "I hope I did not upset you too much."

"No, I was only concerned for your safety is all. I'm glad you are OK. I almost showed up to your house; I won't lie."

"My house—you know where I live?" she asked, puzzled. "I'm fine. Really. I only needed a few more things, most importantly my laptop. I am not scared of him, Baron."

"I do know where you live. I looked over your résumé with Martin. And maybe you should be scared of him." His tone was firm once again. "I apologize for that; I'm just still processing all of this."

"No, I understand." She looked down at the floor.

"Well, did he try to stop you from leaving?"

"Not physically, if that is what you're asking. He begged for understanding and forgiveness."

Just as he set his water bottle down on the coffee table, his phone rang. "Let me take this. Please excuse me, Katherine."

Kathrine fiddled with her phone while Baron disappeared into his room on his cell. She started to clean out her text messages and emails, wasting time. As she scrolled down, deciding which texts to keep and which to trash, she spotted Amy's name. Instantaneously, she became irritated and angered. She had yet to confront or deal with Amy and was unsure if she ever would. She wasn't sure what she would even say to her. *What could I say? "How dare you"? What good would it do? What would it accomplish?* she thought. She envisioned slapping Amy so hard across the face that it stung her hand. The thought made Kat feel good. Maybe she would confront her eventually, when things settled down.

Baron walked back into the living room with his cell clutched tightly in his hand, which hung down by his thigh. His face was ghostly white, and his eyes were bloodshot red. He stood there in silence, staring at Kat.

Kat stood up slowly. "What is it?"

He walked to the couch, appearing lost, as if he were a zombie. He had no expression upon his face, only pale skin and a blank stare. As he sat, she noticed a tear fall from his eye. He didn't attempt to wipe it away.

"Baron, what is it?" she asked again.

"They found her. They found Sophia," he whispered as more tears fell like a waterfall from his face. He did not ugly cry; his cry was graceful and gentle. He laid his cell phone down on the table and placed his elbows on his knee and his face in his hands, trying to hide his tears now.

Kat fought back tears of her own. She felt deeply sad for him. "I'm so sorry, Baron. Is she dead?" she asked softly as she sat beside him, attempting to console him. She wrapped her arms around him and pressed her face into his shoulder. They sat close for what felt like an eternity without saying a word.

After a few silent minutes passed, he looked at her with sad eyes. "I have to go identify her body." Sophia's family had returned to Madrid, and Baron was left to make the dreaded trip to the coroner alone.

Kat grabbed his hand. "I will go with you, Baron. You don't have to do this alone."

Kat wanted to ask Baron how she'd died and where they'd found her, but she knew better. It wasn't the right time. As they gathered their things and headed out, silence and despair filled the air. Kat held Baron's hand for the entire trip. She hurt for him. She knew the pain from losing Noah.

As they arrived at the morgue, Kat stayed back and took a seat in lobby area. The room was cold and scary. There was no color; gray, white, and black filled the room. She sat alone and waited for him to return.

As she sat, her cell rang. She recognized the number but could not recall whose number it was, so she let it go to voice mail. She did not have the energy to hold a conversation at the moment. Her insides were twisted. All the hate she'd had for Sophia had dissolved, and she now felt sadness for her. She hadn't deserved to die. She had made a mistake, not one worth dying for. Kat was lost in thought, contemplating what had happened to her. She wanted to hold on to the belief that Ryan would not have and could not have hurt her or killed her. *No way.* She did admit to herself that Ryan was no longer the man she had known. Was it possible he'd killed her? She was second-guessing her certainty.

Baron reappeared. He no longer looked sad and empty; he reappeared angry. The color in his face had returned—red. He moved toward her sternly. "Let's go," he said as he motioned toward the door. He held the door open for Kat as they made their way out to the busy street.

"Baron, wait," Kat said, trying to keep up with him. He was walking quickly and did not turn around, but he did stop. As she approached him, she grabbed his hand once again and hugged him tightly. "Baron, what can I do? I'm sorry this happened. I want to be here for you."

He reciprocated the hug. "This isn't your fault. I'm angry, Katherine. I'm hurt. I don't have the words for my sister. This will kill her."

They returned to Baron's apartment. Kat ordered in Chinese food and tidied up the kitchen while Baron hid away in his room. On the subway ride home, Baron had barely spoken a word. She decided to give him time to process and not push him for answers. She wanted to know the details. She did not want to read about it in the paper. She thought about Ryan again. Did he know? Was he OK? Had he murdered his mistress? So many thoughts swarmed Kat's mind. How would she go to work tomorrow? How could she possibly focus? Should she stay with Baron? It was all overwhelming.

Baron emerged from his room. He had showered and had clean clothes on, with a clean shave. His face was no longer white or red, just pink. His eyes remained bloodshot—from tears, she supposed. He sat across the room from Kat. "Chinese food?"

"I hope that's OK with you," she replied.

"It's perfect. I'm starved. I know I need to eat. It's been one of the worst days of my life. I can't believe she is gone."

They sat down at the bar and began opening the to-go boxes filled with chow mein and orange chicken.

"I called my sister," he said without looking at Kat.

"Oh, Baron, I know that was difficult for you and for her. I know how it feels to lose a child or a loved one all too well. Not a day goes by that I don't think of Noah. I really hurt for her and you, Baron."

"Thank you for being here, Katherine. Part of me is relieved they have found her. Not knowing was unbearable for my sister and her family." He had stopped shuffling around his takeout. It looked as if he were focused on fighting back tears.

"I understand that. I am here for you. From the moment we met, there was something drawing me toward you. I hate that this has happened, but I am thankful I can be here for you. If I can do anything to help you or your family, please let me."

Baron stood from the barstool and walked toward her. "That means a lot to me, Katherine. Thank you," he said as he wrapped his arms around her.

She felt a tear hit her shoulder. Nothing more was said that evening after dinner. They silently lay together on the couch, mindlessly watching an old movie, until Baron finally said good night, made his way to his room, and closed his door behind him.

At some point during the night, Baron emerged from the bedroom. Kat had fallen asleep on the couch, only to be woken by Baron towering over her.

"I am hurting, Kat. I feel empty. I'm so glad you're here," he whispered. He leaned down and pressed his lips to Kat's. He guided his hands and arms around her waist and lifted her from the couch. He kissed her intensely while jolting her body against his.

Kat wrapped her legs around his waist, not fighting him off. She could feel his excitement against her, and her hand quivered nervously as she slid it down his pants. He was still holding her on his waist, making his way to his bedroom. He tossed her onto the bed and followed. He ripped down her pants forcefully, never removing his lips from her body. Kat felt paralyzed, unable to move. He consumed her, leaving nothing untouched. The heat radiated between their bodies. Baron stretched across Kat, and she felt as if her air supply were cut off; her body throbbed in anticipation of him.

"You want me to stop?" he asked, although he stopped nothing. He held her nipple between his fingers as he asked.

"No," she replied.

He did not stop. Nothing about what they were doing made sense that night, but she wasn't ashamed. She yearned for him, and she gifted herself the pleasure of him that evening without hesitation. Baron needed the distraction that night.

TWENTY-TWO

The next morning, Kat woke next to Baron. She had managed to set her alarm for work. She rolled over and draped her arms around him, touching her lips to his ear. "Good morning," she breathed.

He rolled over with a smile on his face. "Good morning."

"Should I stay here with you today? I hate to leave you alone with this," she said.

"No, Katherine, go to work. I'll be OK. I have some things to arrange, and I will be on the phone all day with my sister. They are planning on flying tomorrow. I wanted to do what I can today, so they are not overwhelmed any more than necessary after arriving."

"I understand." She paused. "Baron, can I ask what happened? Or do they know? If you're not ready to talk about it, I get it."

"Can we talk about it later, Katherine? I think that would be best. Go to work, and try to distract yourself, OK?"

"Sure," Kat responded. She dreaded going to work and listening to the office gossip about Baron or the tragedy. No one knew she was staying with him, which was best. She was also unsure if anyone else knew yet. What had Baron told Mr. Merrill? She would soon find out.

Katherine left for work. As she sat on the subway, she felt her phone vibrate in her bag. She saw another voice mail from a number she vaguely recognized—the number that had called the prior day. She decided to listen to the message when she got to work. She had another voice mail, this one from Ted Thompson, Ryan's coworker. *Not now.* What had he told everyone?

Kat walked into the office, which was surprisingly quiet for a Monday morning. Libby was sitting at her desk, as usual, with the phone against her ear. She waved at Kat and then lifted her mug and pointed, as if asking Kat if she wanted coffee. Kat gave her a thumbs-up and hurried into her office to prepare for the Monday meeting.

Once again, the conference table was crowded as people bantered back and forth about their weekends to one another. No one seemed to know what had transpired with Baron's niece. Kat could have blown their minds by sharing her weekend, but she decided not to. Just then, Mr. Merrill walked in. He sat with a red face. She could tell he was about to share some bad news; she saw it in his face.

He did. He announced to the room that Baron's niece had been found deceased. Baron would be out for a few days. He asked that the team give Baron some privacy for the moment. Speculation and whispers shot through the room after Mr. Merrill left the room. They opted out of the regular Monday morning discussion, as everyone seemed to be in shock. People went missing all the time in New York, but it never was anyone you knew. Baron was well liked throughout the office. It appeared people were genuinely saddened by the news for Baron and his family.

Kat returned to her office to find a mug filled with coffee sitting on her desk. She phoned Libby.

"Yes, Mrs. Letty?" Libby answered.

"Thank you for the coffee," she replied.

"Of course, dear. Guess you heard they found Baron's niece, huh?" Libby almost muttered through the phone.

"I did. Just awful. Heartbroken for him and his family."

"Wonder what happened to her. I heard she was pregnant. A friend of a friend's daughter knew her pretty well."

Kat couldn't find words; she was trying to make sure she'd heard Libby correctly. "Pregnant?"

"Yes, Tammy's daughter—my friend's friend—said Sophia had told her she was pregnant. What a tragedy, huh? Terrible. She was so young and such a sweet girl. I can't imagine anyone wanting to hurt her. Just a shame. Got to go; someone is here. Looks like cops." Libby hung up on Kat.

Kat sat there holding the phone still in her hand. *Pregnant. She was pregnant?* Surely that was not true.

Libby peeked her head through the doorway. "Mrs. Letty—Kat, I mean—you have some visitors," she said curiously.

"Visitors? Who is it, Libby?" she asked.

Her eyes widened. "They didn't say. They just need to speak with you, they said. Pushy gentlemen." Libby rolled her eyes. "Should I send them back?"

"Sure, thank you," Kat replied.

Just as Kat suspected, it was Detective Ferguson, and he'd brought along another gentleman, who was much younger. "May we come in?" Ferguson asked before breaking the barrier into her office.

"If you must." She stood and motioned them to the chairs in front of her desk.

"I am sure you remember me, Mrs. Letty. This is my new partner, Jade Tucker."

She looked at Jade and then back to Ferguson without acknowledging the introduction. "Why are you showing up to my work, Detective?" she asked. "I'm sorry. I don't mean to be impolite; I'd just rather not beat around the bush. The circumstances we met under in our last meeting were rather stressful for me."

"I agree, Mrs. Letty; they were. I think you will want to come to the station to have this next conversation. I have left you a few voice mails. I had no choice but to come to your office."

"If you need to divulge that you have found Sophia, I am aware. And I am saddened and heartbroken by this. But like I told you before, I can't help you. I don't know anything about what happened to her."

"No, Mrs. Letty, that is not why we are here. Like I said, you should really come to the station. This is not a conversation you want to have here. I am sorry I offended you before, but understand I have a job to do. I work for the victims and their families, and sometimes being offensive comes with the territory. So please come to the station."

The officers stood.

Ferguson adjusted his pants and belt and walked toward the door. He turned and looked at her. "See you shortly." He nodded and walked out. His partner never spoke a word, only followed Ferguson out.

Once again, Kat felt a blanket of fog cover her brain. She faced one nightmare after another. Why had Ferguson been so persistent to see her at the station? Kat felt the urge to vomit, which was not unusual when she felt extreme anxiety. The vomit tickled the bottom of her throat, trying to push its way through. She fought it, and although it remained lodged there, she won. She didn't puke. She grabbed her purse and explained to Libby that she would be back later. Although she wasn't sure she would be, that conversation was easier to have. Libby asked her who the gentlemen were, and Kat told her she would explain later. That seemed to suffice.

TWENTY-THREE

Kat hailed a cab to the station. She was oddly familiar with the station. She felt like Phil Connors in *Groundhog Day*. *Please wake up*, she told herself. *Please just wake up*. She had the same awful anxiety day after day.

A tall gentleman dressed in uniform approached the desk. "May I help you, ma'am?" he asked.

"Detective Ferguson is expecting me. Thanks."

"Follow me." He motioned for her to follow.

He didn't take her to the cold interrogation room she had been in before. Instead, he took her to what appeared to be his office. He had boxes scattered throughout the room; it looked chaotic to Kat. She assumed it was well-organized chaos. The officer motioned for her to take a seat.

"Please, Mrs. Letty, take a seat."

The officer knew her name. She was a little embarrassed by that. "Thank you," she said as he left the room. The door remained open. She could hear chatter up and down the hallway and the squeaking of shoes against the tile. The sound was like nails on a chalkboard to Kat; her patience was wearing thin. She was light-headed and thirsty.

Just then, Ferguson rounded the hall; she heard his voice,

and the sound of his feet dragging along the tile was amplified. He rounded the doorway and rushed in attentively.

"Can I please have some water?" Kat immediately asked.

Ferguson was followed by his partner, Jade, once again. Ferguson looked at Jade and signaled for him to grab some water. "Of course. Thanks for coming."

Kat did not respond. She sat there and waited on her water. She felt weak and embarrassed, with glassy eyes. She wanted to cry, puke, and pass out all at the same time. Unfortunately, that had become a typical feeling for her lately. She had no idea why she was there. She didn't feel comfortable sitting there with a stranger who'd all but accused her of killing someone previously.

"Mrs. Letty, when was the last time you spoke with your husband, Ryan?"

"Yesterday. Wait—the day before yesterday. I don't know, Detective. These last few days have been all so much." A single tear rolled down her face.

He reached over and handed her a tissue. "I understand the emotional toll all this has taken on you. But it is important. Have you seen him in the last twenty-four hours?"

"Yes, I did see him yesterday. I went to the house to grab some things," she said. "Why are you asking me this? Is he in some trouble?"

Detective Tucker entered the room and handed Kat her water. She gulped the water as if she had been stranded in a desert for days without water. Tucker took a seat beside her. His eyes fixed on her, as if he knew something bad was coming for her.

"Mrs. Letty, we found Ryan in your home last night dead. He apparently took his own life."

Kat jumped out of her seat and became hysterical, sobbing

and pacing. Tucker stood alongside her, not touching her but standing with her, never saying a word.

Detective Ferguson stood as well. "I am very sorry, Mrs. Letty. He made a phone call last night to a friend, Tom. Tom said the phone call was strange, and he was concerned about Ryan, so he went over to check on him. Again, I'm very sorry. Tom then called 911, but unfortunately, it was too late to save him."

Kat continued to sob. "Why? Why would he kill himself? I don't understand any of this!" she shouted.

"He was being investigated for the murder of Sophia Gantz. I'm not implying he was guilty, as he's innocent until proven guilty, but he was aware we were planning on charging him. Ryan had connections. I spoke with him yesterday."

"I can't do this right now, Detective. Please. I just can't." She knelt down on the floor, struggling through her tears and runny nose, searching for her purse she had set down. She still felt woozy but even worse now. "I just need to go home and lie down, please."

"You can't go home. It's restricted access, Mrs. Letty. Give us some time."

"Give *me* some time. I can't even comprehend what is happening. Ryan would never kill someone or himself. This is all insane. I have to go—now." Kat sensed the denial roll off her tongue. She knew Ryan had changed, but she was not ready to face reality. She threw her bag over her shoulder and trudged out of the room, still bawling.

She knew she had to return to work to explain to Mr. Merrill what had happened. If she had any chance of keeping her new job, she would have to face it head-on. She could not start over once again. She pep-talked herself into heading back to her office. Before leaving the station, she stopped in the restroom and washed her face with wet paper towels. She sat on the commode for a few minutes, making sure she had the nerve.

"Mr. Merrill, can I have a word?"

"Of course, Katherine. Are you OK?" He stood as he asked. He looked concerned.

Kat wondered if the noticeably red face and bloodshot eyes had given away that she was clearly not OK.

"Come on in, and shut the door behind you."

She did as she was told. She sat across from him. "Mr. Merrill, I have received some devastating news today. I will need some time off. I know this is an inconvenience, as I've only just started this job." She wiped away a stray tear that had managed to escape.

"What is going on, Katherine? Devastating news? Are you ill?"

"No, sir, my—" She began to cry again. "I'm sorry," she said as she wiped away her tears with her hands. "My husband has committed suicide." She could barely finish the sentence.

"Oh, Katherine. Oh my." He stood from his chair and walked around the desk to hug Kat. He patted her back a few times. "Please, yes, of course, take some time." He walked back around to his chair. He sat and gazed at Kat from across the desk. "This office has had some real tragedy in the last few days. I am just so very sorry to hear this. You and Baron both have had some dreadful news this week. You will be in my prayers. If there is anything else I can do to help, please let me know. Come back when you're ready. I am grateful to have you on our team. I am so very thankful Baron recommended we reach out to you for this position. You are such an asset to this company, so take all the time you need."

"Baron recommended me?" she asked as she wiped her nose with a tissue from Mr. Merrill's desk.

"Indeed, he did. He said he knew your husband and had

researched your work. It was only fate that a week later, you sent us a résumé. Otherwise, we would have eventually reached out to you. Again, anything you need, please don't hesitate to ask. Now, go home."

Kat left Mr. Merrill's office and headed to the restroom. She went into a stall, climbed onto the commode, and lifted her feet. She curled up and continued to cry. She was amazed she had any tears left to cry. She heard the door creep open.

"Kat?" Libby whispered.

"Yeah?" She snorted, grabbing some toilet paper to wipe her nose.

"You OK, honey?" Libby asked, concerned.

"Yeah, I'm fine. I just need a minute is all."

"Did something happen, darling? Can I help you? I noticed you looked as if you had been crying when you came back. Let me help you, please, honey. What can I do?"

"Nothing. No one can help me, Libby. Thank you. I'll be fine. I just need to be alone. I am leaving, and I will be off for a few days, OK? Just leave my messages on my desk, if you don't mind," she said through the stall. Kat could see Libby's feet at her stall door now.

"I sure will, but if you need anything else, please let me know."

"Thank you. I will."

Libby left the bathroom. Kat soon followed; she rushed to her office, grabbed her bag, and left. Luckily, few colleagues were in their cubicles. She was able to escape without anyone but Libby spotting her.

As Kat approached the exit, she wondered how Baron knew Ryan. That had been a confusing conversation. Baron never had mentioned knowing Ryan, and she recalled introducing them at dinner one evening before beginning at the *Daily*. They had not seemed to know each other. Why would Baron have told Mr.

Merrill he knew Ryan? She was puzzled. She decided to head to Baron's, wondering if he was there. She figured he was running errands for his sister, and she began to feel guilty for not calling him with the news of Ryan's suicide already.

When Kat arrived at Baron's, the door was unlocked. She called out for Baron but received no answer. He was not home. She was somewhat thankful, as she felt exhausted and sick and wanted to lie down. Her body felt as if it were going to give out at any moment. Every step took effort. She needed sleep. She needed her dark hole that she was comfortable in. She powered her cell off before climbing into bed.

She dreamed of Ryan in her sleep. She dreamed she, Ryan, and Noah were in the park, having a picnic, just as she had envisioned many times while pregnant with Noah. Things were as they should have been in the dream, only for Kat to wake up to reality and a migraine.

She wasn't sure of the time, but her room was dark. The sun had set, so she knew it had to be at least eight o'clock, as it was early September in New York. The sun set at about seven thirty each evening. She powered her phone back on and saw that it was 8:58 p.m. She could hear the TV on in the living area. Baron was home. He had not disturbed her, and she wondered if he knew she had left work early to come home. She slipped on some joggers and a sweatshirt over her T-shirt. She looked in the mirror; her eyes were still puffy and swollen from the day's events. She wiped away the leftover mascara still parading around her eyes and threw her hair back in a headband.

"Hey," she said as she surfaced from the guest room to see him sitting on the couch with a glass of wine in hand.

"Hey," he responded, patting the seat next to him, inviting her to come sit. "Would you like a glass of wine?"

"No, thank you." She sat close to him. "I was visited by two detectives today about Ryan," she said. "They came to my work."

Baron looked up at her and set his glass down in front of him. He leaned in toward her, as if beckoning her to continue. He laid a hand across her knee gently.

"Ryan killed himself." She began once again to cry.

Baron hugged her. He did not say a word; he only wrapped her up and held her tightly as she wept.

"Does this mean he's guilty, Baron?" she muttered while she sobbed. She laid her head in his lap and clutched a pillow against her body. "Why else would he do this?"

Baron rubbed her hair and her forehead gently. "Katherine, I don't know. I did know they were going to file charges. I didn't tell you, because I did not want to hurt you. I was planning on telling you, but I was waiting for the right moment."

"But how did they know it was him? Please tell me, Baron."

"They had evidence, Katherine, in her apartment. They have been searching for her body, and once they found it, they were going to move forward. Apparently, he killed her there in the apartment, but they needed to find her. I don't want to hurt you, but you need to know. She was pregnant with his child. They found a letter she had written to him torn up in the bottom of the trash."

Kat sat back up. "She was pregnant?"

"Yes."

"How do they know it was his? And even if it was his, I mean, to murder her? I'm sorry, but I just can't imagine him being violent or murdering someone. I lived with him for years, and he was never violent. He didn't even have a temper. I'm shocked is all." She was no longer sobbing; she was stunned and baffled.

He choked back tears, and his voice began to crack. "He

strangled her, put her in a suitcase, and left her in Suffolk County, in the Central Pine Barrens. A farmer found her. Apparently, some wildlife rummaged through the suitcase, exposing her, which led to her body being discovered. I am sorry about the details, Katherine, but you have a right to know. Soon enough, it will be all over the news, I'm afraid."

Kat sat there in disbelief, trying to grasp the news Baron had just shared with her. "What did her letter say? What did she write?"

"Why do you need to know that, Katherine? It will only hurt you more."

"Because I want to know. Do you know what it said?"

"I do."

"Please tell me, Baron."

"Apparently, she had a visit from Amy—your friend Amy. Amy threatened to tell you about her if Sophia did not end it with Ryan. Sophia pleaded with Ryan in the letter to tell you himself and said that if you didn't, then Amy or she would tell you. She expressed in the letter that she wanted to raise the baby with him and give him the child back that he'd lost, the family he yearned for. If he didn't, she planned on keeping the baby anyway. It's a lot to take in, Katherine. I am so sorry. We are both hurting right now. Can we talk about this later? It is making me ill, talking about it."

Kat sighed. "Yes. I don't feel wonderful either. I believe I need a walk. Would you excuse me?" She rose from the couch.

"A walk? Katherine, it is almost ten o'clock at night. Don't you think it's a little late for a walk? It's dangerous. I'll go with you if you insist."

"No, I would like to be alone. I will be fine. I insist," she said firmly.

CHAPTER

TWENTY-FOUR

Kat threw on her Nikes and went out to greet the city lights, the soaring buildings, the streets filled with parked cars along the curbs, the buzz of cabs' horns, and the bricks that lined the sidewalks. She took several deep breaths in and out. The smell of the city put her at peace, if only temporarily. She took off down the street; she had become a bit familiar with the area since staying with Baron. It was nice, and she felt safer on this walk than she had in weeks.

Some shit has gone down, she thought. She couldn't believe Ryan was gone. She was still angry at him for all the mistakes he had made. He had cheated, lied, and possibly committed murder, although she was not 100 percent convinced that was true. But she still loved him. Part of her always would. She had met Baron and had unexpected feelings for him. How had it been any different for Ryan? She scolded herself silently. She wished she had one more opportunity to tell Ryan that she did indeed love him, despite everything. She never once had thought that would be the last time she saw him. She was just no longer in love with him. She could only take so much. She told herself she was fortunate to have Baron through all of this; it had to be fate.

The lights were beautiful that night, even the streetlights. The city was busy, with people emerging on the streets from every door. She wondered if she would ever feel normal again. How lucky all those people were, wearing smiles and seeming to have no cares and no burdens weighing them down. She envied them.

She looked at her phone: 11:48 p.m. She hopped onto the subway and headed toward Chelsea. She wanted to see her home. She knew she couldn't go in, but she wanted to see it. It once had held so many dreams of hers—so much of what could have been and what should have been. She thought about Tom. *How awful to find your friend dead.*

She picked up her cell phone and sent him a text: "Tom, can we talk? Please call me tomorrow. I'm sorry about Ryan. I loved him so much. I really need to talk."

Immediately, her phone buzzed. Tom wrote, "Yes, let's talk. Now?"

She responded, "Now is perfect. Where?"

Tom wrote, "My place."

Tom lived near her house, so she rerouted and headed to Tom's. Kat had been to Tom's house many times with Ryan and Amy for pizza, beer, and football back before life had become so muddled. They had stayed up late, playing charades and laughing.

She arrived at Tom's place. He had a nice little loft in the West Village. Tom's parents were wealthy and always made sure he was taken care of. She knocked gently. It was weird to be there without Ryan.

Tom answered the door. He looked beat. He instantly hugged Kat before saying a word. "Come in, Kat." He wasn't smiling. His face was heavy and burdened.

"Tom, I'm so sorry you had to find Ryan like that. I can't

believe this has happened." She followed him into the kitchen. The loft was small and messy. The dishes were piled up, overfilling the sink.

"You want a beer? I have those girlie beers if you want one."

"Sure, Tom. Thank you."

"Have a seat." He gestured at the chair next to his.

It was now late into the night—it was early morning, actually—so Kat sent Baron a text: "Hey, I'm with a friend. I'm OK. Please don't wait up."

Tom spoke. "You moved out, Kat? Man, what happened? What was going on? He called me that night, talking crazy." His voice was shaking.

"Tom, some things happened; I don't know what all you know. I do know you two were close and spent a lot of time together, but I am not sure what all he shared with you."

"About the affair?" he asked.

"So you did know?"

"Well, he started skipping out on me. Didn't show up to work out and would tell me, 'If Kat asks, I was working out with you.' So I mean, I figured he was having an affair." He hung his head. "I'm sorry, Kat. Wasn't my business to tell, and he was my friend. I hope you can understand that."

"I am not upset at you. I do understand. Did you tell Amy he was having an affair?" Kat asked.

"Yeah, but she swore she wouldn't tell you."

Kat knew that was how Amy had found out about Sophia. She could see the hurt in Tom's eyes and decided not to mention Ryan and Amy's situation. She didn't want to tarnish the friendship he believed he and Ryan had shared. Although part of her wanted to wound Amy, she decided it would upset Tom more than it would hurt Amy. He had already found Ryan dead; she couldn't add to that misery.

"Amy didn't tell me, Tom. I found out on my own. I left him for it. I had returned that day to gather some more of my things. He was upset about me leaving, but I never imagined he would hurt himself, much less kill himself. I did still love him; I hope you know that."

"Yeah, I know. He loved you too, you know. I think he was lonely, Kat. That's all. He was saying some crazy shit on the phone, though. He said, 'Tell Kat I didn't hurt her. Tell her I am sorry. Tell her I love her and that I never loved anyone more than her.' He hung up on me and wouldn't answer my calls. He was crying, almost hysterical. Never heard him like that before. Not even when Noah—" He paused. "I'm sorry, man." He shook his head and began crying silently. "I should have been there; I should have gotten there quicker."

Kat stood up and hovered over Tom, placing her arms around him. "Tom, this isn't your fault."

They sat in silence for a few minutes. Then Tom got up and grabbed another beer. "What was he talking about, Kat? Why was he saying all that shit?"

"It's a long story. He didn't hurt anyone, or at least I'm not absolutely convinced he did. He was about to be charged with murder. The girl he was having an affair with went missing. The police found her dead and, well, pregnant with what was apparently Ryan's baby."

"Jesus Christ, Kat."

"Yeah. I know."

"Why do they think Ryan killed her? He wouldn't kill anyone. I mean, I know him; I've known him for most of my life. No way he was capable of something like that."

"That is what I said. Sophia, the girl who was murdered—her uncle works with me. He said they had evidence, a letter threatening to expose him. I don't know what else. When the detectives called me in to tell me about Ryan committing suicide, I was too devastated to even ask questions. They were the investigators on her death, and I'm assuming that's why Ryan's case was handed to them. I'm really not sure. I am unsure if they would have divulged any details to me anyway."

Tom sat there in disbelief, just as Kat had. "Have you talked to Amy?" he asked. "We broke up, and she isn't taking my calls right now. I even tried to reach out after I found Ryan, and she wouldn't answer. I figured she knew, though, if you knew."

"We aren't talking either, Tom. I guess we broke up too. It's another long story for another day, though." Kat couldn't bear to tell Tom that Ryan had slept with Amy. In some twisted way, Tom did love Amy. He was unfaithful and obnoxious, but he did care for Amy deeply. He just never managed to do right. Plus, knowing Ryan had been disloyal and slept with his girlfriend would just taint the memories he had of their friendship. She left it alone again.

"Did he say anything else, Tom?"

"I don't know. I couldn't understand half of what he was saying. I think he had been drinking. The cops said maybe he had already taken the pills, and they were kicking in. He was slurring. He said, 'She will know where to find it.' I don't know what that means."

Kat never had asked how Ryan had done it. She hadn't been sure she could handle it. But there it was: he had taken some pills and overdosed. It hit her right in the gut, and she lost her breath briefly. She wondered if Ryan had tried to call her. She powered her phone off so frequently that she most likely never knew if he did try to call her. She felt a sudden wave of guilt. Could she have stopped him? What if her phone had been on? Had he even tried to call her? Her face suddenly felt flushed. She could feel the warmth penetrating her cheeks.

"I'm not sure either. Tom, would it be OK if I crashed on your couch tonight? I don't feel all that well, and I'm just tired. I just hit a wall. I apologize."

"Of course you can. I'm going back to work in the morning, so it's all yours." He looked her straight in the eye, grabbed her hand, and patted it. "Kat, I'm really sorry. He was a good man. You're a good woman. You'll be OK."

Kat could tell he was slightly drunk. "Thank you, Tom. Now, go get some rest. I have kept you up long enough."

"OK, night. The blankets are in the basket by the TV; help yourself."

Tom roamed off to bed, leaving Kat alone with her thoughts.

CHAPTER
TWENTY-FIVE

Kat awoke to the sun beaming onto her face through the window. The warm sunshine felt good on her skin. She checked her phone, and two missed calls from Baron presented across her home screen, along with another from an unknown number. She rubbed her eyes and anticipated the day's events; she would be arranging Ryan's funeral that day. She was to meet with the funeral director to discuss details. She had seen death many times, yet it wasn't any easier this time. She was full of regret about leaving Ryan that last time as he sat there pleading. Maybe she should she have stayed, she thought. But she knew better. *Stop it, Kat,* she told herself. *This is not your fault.*

Ryan had had many friends; she was certain her answering machine at home was full of messages, with her mail running over. She needed to return home. She decided she would pay Ferguson a visit that day to see if she could go back to the house now.

Tom had evidently already left the house for work that morning. He'd left a note for Kat on the coffee maker: "Please make yourself at home. I didn't want to disturb you. We will talk soon. Tom." Kat made some coffee and made her way to the bathroom. The bathroom was messy. She managed to find one clean towel in the cabinet. She washed her face and placed some toothpaste on her finger. *This will have to do.*

She left Tom's place and hailed a cab to the precinct to find Detective Ferguson. As she arrived, she met him exiting the building.

"Mrs. Letty, how are you?" he asked.

"Making it, I guess. Listen, I came to see you, actually. Can I go home yet?"

"I was planning on calling you. Yes. We have released your home; it's no longer restricted access, so you may go home. I still need to sit down with you, though. I have a few questions I need to ask."

"I understand. Today I am planning my husband's funeral. Can I have a little more time?" she asked gently as her voice trembled. She found herself fighting back another waterfall of tears.

"Of course." He reached out a hand to hers. "I'm sorry about your loss, Mrs. Letty."

She let herself shake his hand this time. It was the first time she'd believed him. He appeared genuinely sympathetic for Kat. She had been through so much in the last few days, and it was written all over her face.

As Kat let go of his hand, she headed toward the subway. She planned on making her way to the house to clean up and shower before meeting the funeral director. On her way, she decided to reach out to Jules. The news about Ryan would be spreading like wildfire soon enough, and she felt Jules should hear it from her.

"Hello?" Jules answered.

"Hi, Jules." Kat immediately started crying.

"Kat? What's wrong? Are you crying?" Jules asked. She could tell from the sniffles she was indeed crying.

"He's gone, Jules. Ryan's gone." She could feel the people on the subway looking at her, but she didn't care.

"What do you mean he is gone?"

"They found her dead, and he killed himself, Jules. He took some pills and killed himself!" Kat was hysterical again. Saying it out loud for the first time upset her to the core. She felt as if someone had grabbed her insides and twisted them into a knot. "How the fuck has this happened?" She was now screaming and uncontrollably wailing.

"Kat, where are you?" Jules asked.

"On the subway. I'm headed to my house," she blubbered.

"OK, wait for me outside the house. Text me the address. I'm coming, OK?" Jules replied.

"OK," Kat responded as she wiped her nose on her jacket sleeve. She had calmed down a little. The thought of having someone there to go into that house with her gave her a shred of relief.

When Jules arrived, Kat was sitting like a child on the curb. Jules sat down on the curb beside her and put an arm around her.

"Hi." Jules spoke softly.

Kat turned her head and looked at Jules. "Hi," she said, placing her head gently on Jules's shoulder. "I'm glad you're here. I really am."

Kat had no one. She had Baron, but guilt made it difficult for her to feel comfortable near him right now. She needed a friend, and Jules knew it.

"Kat?" Jules said. "Can I ask you a question?"

"What is it?"

"Did Ryan do it here?"

"Yeah. He did," she responded as her eyes met the ground. They were still sitting on the curb.

"Are you sure you're ready? I mean, I don't mind going in, but you don't have to, Kat."

"I'm OK with going in. I want to go in. Really, I'm fine with it. I just have so many regrets. I'm so confused and hurt. I really just need to talk about it, I think."

As Jules grabbed Kat's hand and pulled her up off the curb, she responded, "OK, well, come on. Let's do this. You can tell me everything."

They stood up and headed inside.

CHAPTER
TWENTY-SIX

The house was disheveled and tossed over. Their things were scattered across the rooms. Old pictures had been thrown across the table. The cabinets had been left open, and dishes had been flipped. It looked like a movie scene in which thieves were in desperate search for a secret map or a jewel, leaving nothing unscathed. Clearly, the police had combed the home. She instantly made her way to Noah's room to check out the damage. It was not bad; a few things had been tousled. She wondered what the police had been looking for. *Evidence? For Sophia's murder or his suicide?* She wasn't sure.

Jules came in behind her. She found Kat cleaning up Noah's room. Jules looked around. "Can I help you, Kat?"

"Sure, just put his clothes back in his drawers, would you?"

Kat had left the room just as it was. Jules had never been inside her home, but it was obvious Kat had not packed up Noah's room or gotten rid of anything. There were still soaps and powder on the shelf of the changing table. Jules got the room put back in order so that Kat would sit down and talk. Jules picked up the baby clothes and began placing them back in the drawers, as Kat had asked.

They spent about twenty minutes replacing all Noah's things.

"That should do it." Kat rubbed her palms together.

"Why don't you shower, and I'll go downstairs and start straightening up the kitchen and make you a snack, OK?" Jules said.

Kat nodded in agreement and disappeared to her bedroom. Jules made her way to the kitchen. She began to put the dishes back into the cupboards and return the silverware and such to their proper places. She finished the kitchen and managed to make Kat a sandwich before Kat made her way to the kitchen.

"Thank you, Jules," Kat said. Kat had showered and washed her hair. She had put on a long-sleeved sweater with jeans. Her hair was still wet and was touching her shoulders, leaving the tops of her shoulder slightly wet. She sat at the bar.

Jules slid over the plate with a sandwich. "You're welcome. Now, eat that, sister."

Kat picked up the sandwich and looked at it. She recalled her last visit home with Ryan; she had encouraged him to eat some toast. She had even made it for him before leaving upstairs to pack more of her things. Her eyes began to well with tears. She wiped them away and took a bite of the sandwich.

As Kat finished her sandwich, Jules vanished to pick up the living room. Kat's phone vibrated. Baron was calling. "Hey," Kat answered.

When Jules reentered the kitchen, Kat was holding her phone against her ear. Kat was uncomfortable, assuming Jules could see her embarrassment. Baron was angry on the other end. Kat's expression remained blank as she attempted to hide the argument from Jules.

Jules tapped Kat's hand and whispered, "You OK?"

Kat nodded and waved her off, miming, "I'm fine."

"Baron, I'm sorry. I'm OK. I stayed with a friend last night, and now she is at my house with me. The police said I could come home." She did not dare to tell him she had stayed at Tom's. "I can go with you if you need me to. I have to meet the funeral director today too about Ryan."

Kat hung up the phone.

"Who in the world was that, Kat?"

"I'm ready to tell you everything," Kat said.

Kat and Jules talked for more than two hours. Kat disclosed everything, leaving not one detail unspoken, starting from the moment she'd discovered Ryan's affair with Sophia. She told of trailing them regularly; Baron, her feelings for him, and running into him a few times; Baron's claim to her boss that he knew Ryan; Amy's multiple lies; Sophia's murder; and her suspicions regarding Ryan at times. She left no stone left unturned. Jules listened carefully the entire time.

"That is a lot, Kat," Jules said. She was speechless. She sat there for a good four minutes before speaking again. "Kat, I think you really need to sit down with this detective guy—Ferguson. Some of this doesn't make sense. It is all so coincidental. I mean, did Ryan really kill himself? I am not trying to scare you, but you don't even know Baron. And Amy leaving Sophia's apartment building? That's pretty damn suspicious."

"I mean, Jules, I can't remember exact dates; this has been a whirlwind since it began. I sound like a mental patient. I am beginning to wonder if I made half this up."

"No one could make this up. And any normal human would feel overwhelmed in this case."

"I couldn't remember seeing Ryan the day before he died. Ferguson asked me, and I wasn't even sure. It's like I am losing my mind. I feel so tormented. I keep thinking I will wake up from this nightmare."

"What did Baron want when he called you earlier?"

"He is going to the funeral home to sign for Sophia's body to be sent back to Madrid to her family. I think he wanted me to go with him. He told me not to, but I feel certain that's why he called. He was upset at me for not coming home last night. It worried him."

"Kat, that isn't your home. He is not your husband or your boyfriend. Yeah, you slept with him—so what? That doesn't mean you answer to him. And what about you? You lost your husband. Did he offer to go with you to make arrangements today? Isn't that what friends do for one another? I'm sorry. I have said too much. I don't know, Kat; you just don't know him."

"No, I get you. I know. It seems I don't know anyone anymore. He has been good to me, though. He really has. If it weren't for you and him, there's no telling what would have become of me at this point."

"Have you talked to Amy about all this? Confronted her about Ryan? Does she know about Ryan? She has been in and out of work, and she looks like a mess. Of course, she doesn't speak to me or really anyone, especially lately. She has been extra angry at me—I'm assuming for telling you about her and Ryan."

"No, I haven't. Not sure if I ever will. If she shows up at Ryan's funeral—well, I can't think about that right now." She shook her head and got up from the couch. "I'd better get to the funeral home, Jules; it's getting late."

"I can go with you, Kat. I don't mind," Jules responded.

"You know, I think I've got this. I needed to talk to someone. You have done enough for today." Kat smiled at her.

"You want me to stay?" Jules asked.

"No, I'm going to grab my things from Baron's and come back home. I have so much to sort out with the bank and the

155

funeral, and I really need to return the twenty-two messages on my answering machine. I think I should. Ryan would expect me to. Talking—or venting—helped. Thank you, Jules. I'd love to do this more—well, minus this circumstance. I just mean talking more. Maybe about you some next time." She winked at Jules and embraced her.

"Of course. Please call me later. I was told once that behind every strong woman is a story that gave her no choice. You are strong, and you have been strong. Don't forget that, OK?"

"I won't."

TWENTY-SEVEN

That evening, Kat made her way to Baron's. He was home, sitting on the couch with the TV and lights off. "Baron?"

"Yeah?"

"Why are you sitting here in the dark?" She sat down beside him.

"Just a long day."

"I wish I could have been there for you today," Kat said as she stroked his hair.

"Me too. I mean, I should have been there for you too," he replied as he looked at her.

She laid her head in his lap. In the dark, they sat there together, saying nothing.

The next morning came. Kat had fallen asleep in his lap, and apparently, he had not moved either. Baron's alarm was buzzing. He moved her head off his lap and stretched his neck back and forth. Kat sat up.

"I am too old to sleep like that." He laughed. "I have a crick in my neck this morning."

"I guess we were extra tired, huh?" she replied.

"I never even woke up, Katherine, so I guess so."

"Why is your alarm set? Are you going back to work?" Kat asked.

"Yes, I have some things to do. The magazine wants to release a story on Sophia's death, and they would like my permission before doing so."

"Oh, OK. I mean, yeah, certainly. I was unaware they were preparing a story on Sophia. Are you planning on going to see your sister soon? I mean for her funeral. Are you going?" Kat asked gently.

"I am. I need to settle a few things for my sister here before I leave. I will probably leave in a few days. You OK with that? You could come with me, Katherine."

"Oh, Baron, I'd love to be there for you. But I have Ryan's—" She paused. "I mean, Ryan died too."

Baron's face flushed red. "He chose to die, Katherine; Sophia didn't. He killed himself because he felt guilty for killing Sophia. There you go! I've said it!" he exclaimed as he stood.

Kat was frightened. She could tell he was angry and rightfully so. He could have been speaking the truth, but even if not, he thought he was. He felt no compassion for the man he believed had murdered his sister's child. She wasn't sure how to respond, so she only stood and walked to the guest bedroom. She concluded the best option for both of them would be for her to get her things and leave. The anguish they were both feeling was no one's fault. She did not want to hurt Baron by responding and saying something she might regret. She gathered her possessions and cleaned up the room before leaving.

As she rolled her suitcase through, Baron stood by the door. "Katherine, I shouldn't have said that."

She could tell he felt embarrassed for saying it. "I understand. I do. The lines are blurry, Baron. I can't see straight either. I think it's best if we take some time—some space. I appreciate you letting me stay with you. You have been such a gracious host."

Baron hugged her. "You're welcome. I agree—we need some time. I do not want or mean to say things to upset you. None of this is your fault. Goodbyes hurt only when the story isn't finished. This one hurts, Katherine."

"It does hurt. It all hurts. I'm still here for you if you need me." She smiled as she rolled her suitcase out the door.

Before heading home, she rolled her suitcase to the station. She decided to take Jules's advice. She sat down for four hours with Ferguson. She unloaded the same information to him that she had to Jules. Now he knew all she knew. He didn't say much; he only scribbled down words on his yellow legal pad. Kat had no idea what he was writing, but he wrote a lot. She decided that her first impression of Detective Ferguson had not been accurate or fair. He was doing his job; he was good at his job and took it seriously. He was a solid man who was an advocate for any and all victims.

Kat soaked in the bathtub for two hours that evening. She counted 248 drips from the immense faucet that loomed over the tub. The constant sound of the drip was calming, the way it hit the water and made perfect little waves reliably. She lost count at 248 when her cell rang. It was sitting across the bathroom, on the charger. She let it ring and go to voice mail.

Kat then began to mentally make a list of people to call tomorrow and errands to run. Ryan had life insurance, although she was unsure of the amount. She also needed to clean out his office. Was she welcome? She wondered. At his office, she wasn't sure how many people knew about their issues or the separation. It was, after all, suspicious even to Kat herself. She'd left him, and he'd died the next day. She decided she wouldn't burden herself tonight with those thoughts—such pointless worries.

TWENTY-EIGHT

Two weeks flew by. The funeral was a blur for Kat. Many of Ryan's friends and colleagues were in attendance. The papers released numerous articles about Ryan. One headline read, "Prime Suspect in Socialite Slaying Commits Suicide," with a picture of Ryan displayed. Kat knew several of the authors responsible for the articles. She understood; it wasn't personal. The public ran with it, but his friends and associates remained devoted. Tom stood by Kat and Jules at the funeral. He would occasionally squeeze Kat's hand, reassuring her that he was there. Amy did not show up. Kat was grateful; she wasn't sure how she would have reacted. Many times during the service, Kat felt faint. She was held up by two people standing strong for her. Baron decided not to come. He had sent Kat a letter in the mail, apologizing. He felt it would be a betrayal to Sophia and his family, which again, Kat understood. It was complicated, just like most things lately. The string of nausea seemed to follow Kat around most days, and she began to wonder if she had an ulcer. She told Jules she would see a doctor soon.

Monday rolled around, and she decided it was time to get back to work. She had taken the life insurance money and paid off her mortgage. She still had plenty left over. She could have quit working for a while if she'd wanted to, but she knew she had better not for her sanity. She needed to move on, start the healing process, and begin rebuilding herself once again. Going back to work only concerned her because it meant facing Baron. He'd assured her in the letter that office gossip had slowed down; they had already moved on to Nora, who apparently had been arrested for disorderly conduct. She was unsure of the details. She had no doubt Libby would fill her in upon her arrival.

Jules had come over during the two weeks numerous times, and they had cleaned and packed up Noah's room. It had been difficult for Kat, but she'd managed to do it without feeling guilty. They had donated Ryan's clothes to Goodwill. She had kept a few old T-shirts, the ones with memories. She slept in those most nights. Jules told her that was just fine. Jules and Kat had lunch regularly. Kat asked about Amy some days, but Jules would give a vague answer and move on quickly. Those two weeks were huge for Kat; she wasn't healed, but she was on the right path. *What's done is done*, she reminded herself often.

Detective Ferguson had contacted Kat a few times with questions, always approaching her considerately. She wasn't sure why. She wondered if he questioned Ryan's guilt. She got the feeling there was more to the story, but she didn't trouble herself with it. *What's done is done.*

⚬⚬⚬

As Kat returned to her office for work after her short leave, Libby greeted her with a smile and coffee. "Welcome back, Mrs.—I mean Kat."

"Glad to be back, Libby. Thank you for the coffee." She reached for the mug.

"They are all in the conference room now. Want me to take your bag and laptop to your office for you?" Libby asked.

"Sure, thank you."

Kat walked toward the conference room. As she moved through the door, she immediately locked eyes with Baron. The room became silent.

Mr. Merrill stood. "Katherine Letty, so glad to have you back. Take a seat, please," he said with a smile as he stretched out his arms toward an empty seat. The seat was directly across the table from Baron.

Baron winked at Kat as she sat. The wink was comforting to Kat. She felt a sense of relief. After the Monday meeting, Baron caught Kat on the way back to her office.

"Martin told me the funeral was nice. You holding up OK? I guess you got my letter?"

"I did. Thank you. The funeral was nice, although to be honest, I don't even remember most of it. It was a rough day, as I'm sure you can imagine all too well. How are your sister and your family?"

"You know—day by day. Listen, I hope you're not too uncomfortable. I mean, working with me. It's not fair to say this, but I think about you every day."

"I am not uncomfortable working with you, Baron. Not at all."

Kat turned around and headed to her office. She grabbed her cell and sent a message to Jules: "All is well. Baron was a complete gentleman. Women staring at me in a meeting—no big deal." She inserted laughing emojis. She felt empowered to be able to joke about the matter. She was done being angry and weak, and this time, she meant it.

"I loved your additions to the Liggins piece. Job well done," Mr. Merrill said as he stuck his head into Kat's office.

"Thank you. I had a chance to look over the emails at home—prepping to come back. Thanks for allowing me all the time. I appreciate it."

"Absolutely, dear. Now, get back to work." He chuckled as he turned around back into the hallway. Mr. Merrill was a nice man. His wife had sent flowers to Ryan's funeral, and they both had attended. His wife was younger than Kat had expected, but she was kind, and Kat felt she had been genuine when she consoled her during the friends and family evening. She would never forget the compassion they'd displayed during her time of need.

After lunch, Kat felt nausea rush over her once again. She made it to the ladies' room just in time. Maybe Jules was right. She conceded; she would call her doctor. If it was an ulcer, she definitely needed treatment; she was throwing up regularly at this point. It wasn't nerves; it had to be an ulcer. She was no longer feeling anxious. She actually felt healthier than she had in an entire year, since the nightmare had begun.

"Dr. Phelps's office. This is Sherrie. How may I help you?"

"Hello. This is Katherine Letty. I need to make an appointment to see Dr. Phelps, please."

"Oh, hello, Mrs. Letty." She paused. "Hold one moment, please."

Clearly, Sherrie had heard Dr. Phelps's patient's husband was a murderer. Kat could hear the nervousness in Sherrie's voice.

"Yes, ma'am, I'm back. An appointment, you said? May I ask for what we are scheduling, please?"

"Of course. I have not been feeling well. I believe I have an ulcer."

"Can you come next Tuesday morning at nine forty-five, Mrs. Letty?" Sherrie asked.

"Yes, thank you."

"Please bring an updated insurance card and a list of current medications, ma'am. See you next Tuesday." Sherrie hung up the phone.

Kat texted Jules, "You win. I made a doc appt for next week." Jules would be proud. She had first recommended counseling, thinking Kat needed to talk to someone other than her. She had felt the nausea was nerve- or stress-related at first, but then she had diagnosed Kat with an ulcer. They had laughed, as Jules had zero background in the medical field. "That's what the symptom checker says, Kat, and it doesn't lie," she had told her with a giggle.

"See you tomorrow, Libby," Kat said.

Libby waved her out the door; she was tied up on a call.

Kat left work and headed to meet Tom. They had made plans to have dinner at one of his favorite spots. Kat knew it was a bar, but Tom loved bar food. Those foods were considered meals in the bachelor world. It would be the first time they had seen each other since the funeral. Tom often sent her texts just to check in on her. It was surprising, as Tom never had struck her as the thoughtful type.

As she entered the bar, Tom rose from his seat and welcomed her with a big hug. "Hey, Kat, it's good to see you. You look good," he said as he stepped away to look her over. "You really do. I'm proud of you."

"Thank you, Tom. I'm actually doing OK. It's been rough, but I wouldn't expect anything else. Rough seems to pursue me around like a hungry stray cat these days," she said as she laughed and tailed him to his table.

They caught up, mostly exchanging stories about work. He shared information about a new project he had been working on and a new blonde who recently had joined the gym. The mysterious new hottie was ignoring his advances, and he probed Kat for advice. Kat enjoyed the mindless chatter. It was a breath of fresh air. No heavy talk prevailed.

Tom walked Kat to the subway station. She said, "This was nice. Thank you, Tom."

"Same time next week?" He looked at Kat.

"Sounds good." Kat took off down the stairs into the station.

Amy's name never came up. She wanted to ask Tom if he had heard from her but decided against it. She figured he would have mentioned it if they were back at it. It wasn't unusual for them to take time-outs from each other. She always had blamed Tom, but Kat now questioned all of Amy's tales. She was a liar, after all.

The ride home was uneventful. As she unlocked the front door, she felt her phone vibrate in her purse. From Baron, the text read, "Hope you had a good day. You look great. Still on my mind."

Kat wasn't sure how to respond. She debated her response. The truth was, he was also still on her mind. She was trying to get healthy and move on from all of it the best she could. She had read in the paper that the police had not actually closed Sophia's case, so Kat could not quite relax yet. She knew Baron was struggling with those same feelings. They were intertwined by the situation. Neither was at fault. She missed having someone around who could relate to what she was dealing with.

"Thank you. It was nice to be back at work. Everyone was so supportive—a good group there. I won't lie to you; I've missed you too." She hit Send.

That night, Kat did something she hadn't done in a while: she prayed. She spent the evening on the rooftop, in Ryan's old Bon Jovi T-shirt, and limited herself to two glasses of wine. It was chilly, but the air felt good and invigorating. She reflected on the happenings over the last year, with only one regret: leaving Ryan that day in that state. She hadn't known how fragile he had become. Although she realized his shortcomings as a husband, she'd failed him that day. Her only comfort was in knowing he was up there with Noah. It put her at peace.

Baron never responded that evening. Kat was OK with it; she wasn't sure where the conversation would have gone anyway.

TWENTY-NINE

Kat threw up twice before heading to work. Her nerves still were not totally right. She still felt apprehension before picking up the paper each morning on her way to work. She passed a small newspaper stand each morning and usually scanned through the paper while riding the subway to the office. She was afraid she would unintentionally be exposed to an article about Ryan, and she was not ready to read it. The media could be brutal. She was paranoid, and she knew it. She convinced herself at times that people had moved on; new stories and new tragedies were already flooding the streets and the papers. She was taking it day to day, and with Jules's and Tom's support, she felt encouraged and resilient. They texted her empowering quotes, stating how strong she was or how she could move on. She appreciated it.

Kat left her office for lunch that day. She had run out of time to pack her lunch that morning and decided to run down to the deli about two blocks from her office. As she read the menu displayed on the wall behind the cashiers, she realized Amy was checking out. Fear and anger rushed her body at the same time, and she instantly turned around and shuffled toward the door. On the way, she dropped her purse, and the contents spilled out.

The gentleman in line behind her helped her gather her things, but she didn't look up; she was panicked. "Ma'am, are you OK?" the gentleman asked.

Kat didn't answer. She just continued to toss her ChapStick and other things back into her purse. She then threw the purse over her shoulder and hurried out the door. She had lost her breath; she was hyperventilating. *Calm down. Calm down*, she repeated to herself. For a split second, she couldn't figure out which way to go. As she turned to her left, she faced Amy, who stood there staring at her. Kat had played out this moment in her head many times, including the things she would say to Amy, but nothing came out. She only returned the glare.

"I loved him, Kat. Just like you did!" Amy bellowed out at her. "I was there for him when you weren't. I was there for you both." She continued to shriek. The street was crowded, but Amy did not seem bothered and continued her rant. She tossed her hand around dramatically, causing a scene. An older gentleman stopped to listen, never interfering.

Kat remained calm. "He didn't love you. He told me. You waited until I was down, when I had no strength to fight, and I trusted you. You are a liar and a fraud. He knew exactly what you were: you were a mistake, a regret. You have no moral compass, and I feel sorry for you."

Amy began to cry, with the tears unleashed forcefully down her face. Her face became flushed and wet, and she turned and walked away.

Kat began to walk the two blocks back to work, feeling brave and empowered. She had left many words unsaid, but she'd said enough. Kat knew those words would sting more than anything else. A smile stretched across her face. *She deserved that*, she thought.

Kat walked boldly back into her office, never missing a beat.

Just then, Baron poked his head in. "Hey," he said as he winked at Kat sitting at her desk.

"Hey," she said.

"How is Katherine today?" he asked.

"You know, I'm good, actually. How is Baron?" she asked as she grinned at him.

"Baron is good too. I was thinking maybe dinner. Can I make you dinner tonight? No tricky stuff, just catching up. Just, I mean, you know, work stuff," he said as he laughed mischievously.

"I would love to, but Jules is coming over tonight. Can I take a rain check? To catch up on work stuff with you," she added playfully.

"Of course," he said as he pulled his head back out of her office. He then immediately returned and said, "Can I add you look beautiful today?"

"Thank you, Baron," she replied as she rolled her eyes at him.

Kat managed to get lots of work done that day. She was making a comeback—a real one this time, she believed.

Kat left the office at five that evening, calling Jules on her way out. She told Jules she had a story for her. Jules agreed to meet her at her house.

Jules was waiting patiently at her door as she arrived home. After settling in and putting on her sweats, Kat melted into the couch next to Jules. Every detail flowed from Kat's mouth about her earlier fiasco with Amy.

"Good for you, Kat. She's just a cockroach," Jules said, and they both burst out laughing.

"A cockroach!" Kat repeated as she continued to laugh.

"Yes, she really is. I hate that I even have to look at her at work. She had that coming. I think you handled it well.

I'm proud of you for standing up for yourself. That deserves a celebratory drink or two," Jules said as she winked at Kat and got up to head into the kitchen. Jules turned around. "We are celebrating your newfound strength. You know, I was once told that it takes a shitload of darkness for a star to shine. Brighter days ahead."

Two glasses turned into two bottles that evening.

⌘

Kat worked her ass off that week. She was nailing it, with each project completed flawlessly.

Mr. Merrill stopped in on Friday. "Impressive week, Mrs. Letty."

"Thank you, sir," she said confidently. "The recharge you allowed me really helped." She smiled as she spoke.

"Have a great weekend," Mr. Merrill said as he exited her office.

As Kat reached for her purse and packed her laptop into her bag, Baron appeared in the doorway.

"So plans for the weekend?"

"Nope, I have none," she said as she looked up at him.

"I'm risking rejection here again, but I must ask. Dinner?" he said as he tucked his hands in his pockets.

"No tricky stuff, huh?" she teasingly asked.

"Oh, no tricky stuff—strictly business. You have managed to put Martin in your back pocket, and I must know your secret. All work. A work dinner," he slyly responded.

"Well, in that case, I accept."

"My house? Or would you like to go out?" he asked. He had made his way closer to her desk. He stood tall, hovering above her in her chair. She could smell him; she could feel the redness presenting from her cheeks.

"Let's eat out. Since this is a business dinner." She smirked at him.

"Out it is. I will be in front of your door at seven o'clock, Katherine. See you then." He saluted her as if he were a soldier and departed from her office.

Kat had two hours to get home, shower, and shave. *Why am I thinking about shaving?* She knew why. She mulled over the thought of ending up in Baron's bed later that evening. She wasn't convinced that was what she needed, but deep down, that was what she wanted.

Kat was greeted at the door at 7:00 p.m. sharp. Baron was dressed in dark jeans and a navy blazer. He wore a white V-neck T-shirt underneath, exposing his salt-and-pepper chest hair. She found his chest wildly erotic. She knew what peeked out at her, just a glimpse of what was underneath. *Is this man cleavage?* She laughed at herself as she pondered. Kat wore a low-cut, long-sleeved, bohemian-inspired black dress. She was small-chested but had managed to place her girls in just the right spot with a max amount of magic tape, as she liked to call it.

"You are trying to seduce me on our work date, aren't you, Katherine?" Baron asked boldly.

"This old thing?" she replied as she looked down at her maxi dress. "I just pulled the first thing I saw out of my closet." She shrugged and laughed.

Baron and Kat exchanged flirtatious comments back and forth all evening. They laughed and conversed for two hours before finishing dinner, never mentioning Ryan or Sophia. Baron was soothing to Kat; it was effortless to be with him.

"What now? I mean, we still need to discuss work, of course. The night can't end yet," Baron said.

"I guess you're right. You tell me," she answered. Kat wasn't ready for the night to end either.

"Let's go dancing, Katherine! When was the last time you danced?" he asked excitedly.

"Dancing? I could not tell you the last time I danced. Maybe at my wedding."

The air suddenly became thick, and neither commented immediately.

"I'm sorry," Kat said. "I—"

Baron interrupted her. "Well, that's too long. We are going to go dancing." He grabbed her hand, and dancing they went.

The night ended with Kat in Baron's bed, just as she secretly had hoped.

❧

The night turned into the weekend. Sunday morning arrived with the sun shining in through the shades.

"Can I take you on a picnic today, Katherine?"

"A picnic would be perfect. As long as you bring a blanket. It's a bit chilly for a picnic!" she exclaimed.

"Sunshine and crisp, fresh air. What else could we ask for?"

"You're right. I'll need to go home to change my clothes. Would you mind?" she asked as she made her way to his bathroom. She grabbed his toothpaste and brushed her teeth as best as she could with her finger. "I also need to brush my teeth!" she yelled out to him.

"I agree," he said as he laughed and walked into the bathroom with her.

She lightly shoved him as she rolled her eyes at him jokingly.

Baron packed up the perfect picnic necessities. He brought her an extra blanket to make sure she stayed warm. The sun was still shining as they lay their blanket out in Central Park.

"This used to be one of my favorite spots, Baron. Ryan and I used to come here a lot when we first started seeing each other." After realizing what she had said, she began to apologize. "I am so—"

He stopped her. "Katherine, don't apologize. Please. I think we should have a serious conversation."

"Yeah, you're right. He is part of me, my past. I don't know what I'm doing. This is all so difficult for you too—I know that."

"Being with you is not difficult; it's quite the opposite. I love being with you. There are no wrong or right questions or answers. We have both had tough circumstances placed at our feet. The lines are gray and blurry. Don't apologize for loving him or for your past. I realize this love story of ours isn't exactly ideal."

"A love story?" she nervously repeated.

"Yeah, Katherine, a love story. I loved you from the minute I met you. I do have a confession, however."

"A confession?" she asked.

"I do hold on to some anger toward Ryan, as you can imagine."

"Yes, I understand."

"But that's not it. Katherine, Sophia told me about Ryan. I knew about you before I even met you."

She sat there stunned, remaining silent.

"You see, I knew she was seeing a married man. Found out who he was, and I researched him and came across you, obviously. My first wife cheated on me too. I felt sympathy for you, and I didn't even know you. I heard your story from Sophia, of course. She told me about you losing your child and your withdrawal from your life. I wanted to intervene, I guess, to save you. If that makes sense. Your résumé was a surprise to me; that was fate. I had already mentioned your name to Martin, hoping he would reach out. Is this too much? I should have told you; I just felt ashamed and intrusive or invasive. I just needed to save you in some disturbed way. Please don't be upset or alarmed by this. I wanted it all out on the table."

Kat sat there on the blanket, processing what he had just revealed to her.

"I don't know what my plan was, Katherine. I just wanted to know you. To be there for you. You were so lovely and so innocent in all of this. And when I met you, well, you were just faultless. I could not understand how he could have done this to you. My hatred for him began there, Katherine. Please say something."

Kat was shaking. She was unsure why. She wasn't scared or upset, only shocked. "This is surprising, Baron. I do feel a bit invaded, I guess. This is strange to me. You knew about them. She confided in you about them."

"Yes, she did." He hung his head in humiliation, tossing around the cheese on his plate uneasily.

"Did she love Ryan? Did she say he loved her?" she asked.

"I don't know, Katherine. Not sure if she knew what love was, to be honest. I think she thought she loved him. Sophia was unique; she was used to getting what she wanted. Katherine, I don't think he loved her. Which upset me for her. He never planned on leaving you; he did tell her that numerous times. She thought the baby would change his mind, but it didn't."

"You said she was with several men—that she had multiple relationships. You told me that. Why was he different? Why did she want him?" Kat asked curiously.

"Again, she was used to getting what she wanted. She could have those other men easily. Ryan was out of reach and, therefore, more enticing. Sounds awful saying that out loud. She did care and maybe even love him. I really couldn't say."

"Do we even know yet for sure that was Ryan's baby she was carrying?" Kat asked.

"Yes, it was confirmed. Detective Ferguson confirmed it. Sophia was young but not dumb. She was careful. I mean, what I'm trying to say is, she wasn't promiscuous. From what she shared with me. I was family; she trusted me. She didn't share her sex life with me in detail, but she would reassure me she was not shaming herself. I took that to mean she was not sleeping around. She felt I fathered her too much, so she tried to reassure me she was not sleeping around, I guess."

"So sleeping with a married man was not shaming herself?" Kat asked heatedly.

"Katherine, I didn't mean that. I know you have hostility—justifiably so. I meant to say she was only sharing her bed with Ryan. She told me the baby was his and that she had not been with anyone else in that way for some time."

Kat began to cry. Baron scooted over on the blanket closer to her. She rested her head on his chest and cried.

They sat in silence for a good ten minutes.

"Not the ideal love story," she said as she looked up and halfheartedly laughed. What else could she do? Neither of them had chosen this; it was what it was. They both lay back and let the sunshine warm their faces.

THIRTY

"Good morning, Libby," Kat said as she strolled by her desk.

"Good morning, Kat."

Kat made her way to the conference room, ready to tackle the week. Monday ended up being dull, with nothing to report to Jules. Kat gave her the rundown on the weekend with Baron. Jules wasn't thrilled, but she tried to be politely supportive. Jules told Kat to be careful and said, "How well do you really know him?" and all the things any friend would have been cautious of. She told Kat she thought Kat needed some time to heal before stepping into another relationship. Kat was grateful for the protectiveness Jules showed. It was nice to know Jules was in her corner. Although Kat somewhat agreed with Jules, she also recognized that tomorrow was not guaranteed.

Kat walked out of work to discover it was drizzling rain and misty. The sun had set. *Great—no umbrella. Where did this come from?* she thought. Someone clutched her shoulder.

"Share a cab?" Baron asked.

"Depends. Where you headed?" Kat said.

"Anywhere as long as it's with you." He smiled and hailed a cab.

"Well, I could use a bite. The salad I brought for lunch is long gone." She hopped into the cab with Baron.

Baron directed the cab driver to a nearby pub.

Kat was wet. Her hair stuck to her head, and her jacket was dripping.

"Let me take that, Katherine." Baron helped her remove her jacket and placed it on an empty barstool next to them.

"Can you excuse me while I go to the ladies' room and stick my head under the dryer?" she jokingly said as she stood back up.

"Sure. But you don't look like a wet dog, if that's what you're thinking. You're kind of sexy with the wet head."

She laughed and headed toward the restroom to clean up.

When she returned, Baron had ordered her a coffee.

"Coffee to warm me up? How did you know?" She winked at him as she sat.

"I'm in tune. I think I have you figured out, Katherine."

"Is that right? Well, thank you. Coffee is perfect."

As they sat there and talked, Kat felt at ease. This was exactly where she wanted to be, with Baron. He was good inside. He was able to overlook the fact that she still had loved Ryan in spite of what had happened. He accepted the forgiveness Kat had granted Ryan.

"Katherine, are you listening to me?" he joked. "I lost you there for a second." He laughed.

"Oh, I was lost in thought. I'm sorry," she said. "I was thinking about how fortunate I am to be sharing this evening with you is all."

"Well, I was actually sharing that thought right out loud to you, and you missed it. Now you'll never know." He shrugged and finished his coffee.

As they left the pub, Baron grabbed Kat's hand and placed it in his. "You have soft hands. I love your hands," he said.

"Thank you." She squeezed his hand eagerly.

They stood outside the pub hand in hand. Bystanders passed along the sidewalk, not knowing what was unraveling right before them.

"Katherine Letty, I'm in love with you. I unapologetically profess. It's a connection I cannot explain. I found something with you that I no longer believed in. I won't apologize for it. I would scream it from the rooftops with no shame."

Kat stopped in her tracks and unconsciously removed her hand from his. "You love me?" she repeated as she looked up at him. It was now raining again, but neither was bothered by the rain, only captivated by the moment.

"I do, and I do know what love is."

"I'm scared, Baron," she said as she reached back out for his hand. They stood face-to-face.

"That makes two of us," he responded. "This is not me saving you. This is more than that. I believe we are saving each other."

The tears Kat cried were different this time. Happy tears were unfamiliar. She spent the night at Baron's again, and without a doubt, he handled her differently that night. She had never felt safer than she did that night.

The alarm buzzed, waking Kat and Baron. "Morning already?" he said as he yawned and stretched. She had stayed over after the love conversation the night before.

"It is," she replied as she rolled over and kissed his lips. "I won't be in until after lunch today. I have a doctor's appointment today at nine forty-five."

"A doctor's appointment?" he asked.

"Yeah, it's just an ulcer, I think. My stomach has been upset for the last few weeks. I wonder why," she said sarcastically. "Jules thinks I need medication." She laughed. "Truthfully, I've been feeling better, but I will go anyway to put Jules's mind at ease." She snickered as she rolled out of bed. "I'll make us some coffee."

Kat headed into the kitchen. Baron's phone was sitting on the charger in the kitchen, when she noticed a text from a familiar number. *That's fucking Amy's phone number*, she thought. There was no name attached to the number. *Why would she be texting him? How does she have his cell?* His phone was locked, so she was unable to read the contents of the message.

She grabbed the phone and marched to the bathroom. She could hear the shower running. "What the hell is Amy texting you for?" she screamed as she entered, holding the phone out as if it were covered in the plague.

Baron opened the shower door. "What?" he asked with a confused look on his face. "Who is texting me?"

"Amy. My friend Amy. I mean my former friend Amy, the one who was sleeping with my husband!" she yelled.

He turned off the shower and stepped out. "Hand me a towel, please," he said, gesturing toward the cabinet to the left. As she handed him a towel, he wrapped himself up. "Katherine, I don't know. What does it say? I don't know Amy."

"It's locked. I can't see it."

"OK, the password is 161616. Open it up. I have nothing to hide. Calm down."

Kat opened the phone and the text. It read, "Everyone knows you did it. They will all find out soon enough."

Kat had half a mind to dash to Amy's house and beat the hell out of her. She was livid. *How dare she! How dare she reach out to Baron.* It wasn't enough that Amy had slept with Ryan; now she was harassing Baron.

"What is she talking about?" Baron asked. "I don't even know her; I have no idea how she has my cell number."

"I have no idea. I'm so mad right now."

"Calm down, Katherine," he said.

"I will not calm down. I'm tired of being calm!" she shouted.

"OK, OK. Get it out," he replied as he dressed. "You know Amy visited Sophia. Threatening to tell you about Sophia."

"Yeah, you mentioned that. The audacity she has! She wanted Ryan to herself. What was her plan? To get rid of me like she did Sophia?"

"Katherine, whoa. That's a huge accusation."

"Perhaps it is, but, Baron, think about it. I don't think Ryan would have hurt Sophia; he wasn't capable of it. I know it." Tears were streaming down her face again.

"I think we should talk about this when you simmer down. Katherine, Sophia was strangled. No way Amy has that kind of strength. I don't want to talk about this right now, OK?"

Kat stormed out of the room. She entered the guest room and went into the bathroom. She locked the door behind her and sat on the commode with her knees up, wrapping her legs in her arms.

Baron gave her about five minutes and then gently knocked on the door. "Katherine, I need to go. Will you come out, please? Let me kiss you goodbye."

Kat reluctantly opened the door.

Baron grabbed her and hugged her. "Give me a kiss. This is just a bump in the road. Don't upset that ulcer," he said as he prodded her in the side and gave her a wink.

She smiled and came out of the bathroom, following him to the front door. "I'm not far behind you. I'll lock up. I'm going home shortly to get ready for my appointment."

"OK, have a good day. I'll see you in a bit." He headed out with his coffee mug in one hand and his briefcase in the other.

Katherine locked up and headed home. She sent Jules a text on the way to let her know what had occurred. Jules had not responded by the time Kat made it home. Kat figured she was on a call or in a meeting.

Kat made it to her appointment right on time. Her eyes were still puffy from that morning. As Kat sat and waited for the doctor to enter, her phone rang. "Hey, Jules," Kat answered.

"What in the actual fuck? Amy sent Baron a text? What does that mean?"

"I don't know. I'm sitting here waiting on the doc. My blood pressure was obviously sky high." She let out a tense, awkward laugh—anything not to cry.

"OK, finish up there, and call me. There is a party tonight at Crazy Joe's Pub, and we are going. It's Halloween. You know that, right? And what else is there to do to blow off steam?"

Kat unwillingly agreed. "OK, sounds good. Can I bring Baron?" she asked as she reflexively bit her lip, hoping Jules would approve.

"Fine with me. Call me later, and we will smooth out the details. Everything is fine. Amy's a cockroach, remember?"

Kat laughed and hung up just as the doctor walked in.

"Mrs. Letty, good to see you again. It's been some time."

Her doctor was an older lady. Kat estimated her to be about seventy. "Dr. Phelps, good to see you. It has been quite a while."

"I have you down for some stomach concerns. You have not had a wellness check in over two years. Can we go ahead and work you up while you're here?" Dr. Phelps asked.

"Sure," Kat said.

"Tell me about the stomach issues."

Kat explained her symptoms. She included the recent event, and surprisingly, Dr. Phelps did not react. Kat was grateful; she couldn't face judgment that day after that morning. Dr. Phelps was professional, and after forty years of practice, Kat was sure she had witnessed some bizarre things. They had a lengthy discussion about Kat's well-being, and Dr. Phelps advised her to see a therapist or counselor—to allow her to vent, not to medicate her. Kat didn't ignore the advice but told Dr. Phelps she was open to it but wanted to think about it.

"Mrs. Letty, although it may very well be stress-related, I'd really like to obtain some labs and go from there. I would also like you to begin an antacid every morning. Take it thirty minutes before you eat. The nurse will give you a list of suitable over-the-counter medications to choose from. I would also like to obtain a urine sample today from you as well. The nurse will be in shortly to discuss the details. It was nice to see you. If you need something, don't hesitate to call my office. I will follow up in a few days with your results."

Kat left Dr. Phelps's office and headed to the *Daily*. She arrived sooner than she anticipated; she made it before lunch. She poked her head into Baron's office. He was on the phone, so she gave him a wave and made her way to her office. With Amy still on her mind, she was grouchy. She closed her door and shut the blinds.

CHAPTER
THIRTY-ONE

Kat watched for the clock to reach 5:00 p.m. *Finally,* she thought. She had not accomplished much that day. Jules was right; she needed a fun night out. Before walking out of her office, she contemplated whether or not she wanted to invite Baron. *Why not? He hasn't met Jules.* Before flipping off her lights, Kat had an epiphany about who she used to be. *Wind me up, and I'll say exactly what you want to hear. I will walk the straight and narrow. I will not take risks. I will sacrifice myself for you. I will appear delicate and always defenseless. I will not rock the boat.* She hardly recognized herself anymore. She was evolving, and it felt terrific. She no longer felt limited or expected to appear a certain way or to always use her manners. She was emotional. She was revived—born again. She would have a night out, and she would bring whomever she wanted.

"Hey, you done?" She peeked into Baron's office.

"I am. You? How was your appointment?" he asked.

"It was fine. I'm fine. I feel better. Thanks. Listen, my friend Jules invited me to a Halloween party tonight. Apparently, it's Halloween." She laughed cynically.

"A Halloween party—does this mean we must wear costumes?" he said as he looked up at her with his glasses on the tip of his nose. He had slid them down to glare at her above them.

Kat thought to herself how attractive and distinguished he looked when he wore his glasses. He sported a slight smile—halfway kidding, she assumed.

"Do you want to wear a costume, Mr. Marco?" she teased.

"Had I been given some time, of course I would, but on such short notice, I'm afraid I will have to go as your hot date." He fired back at her provocatively.

"A date it is. I shall send you details shortly. You get to meet my friend Jules. You will love her."

He slid his glasses back up and nodded. "I'm right behind you. See you tonight, Katherine."

Kat rang Jules for the details. Jules was dressing as a slutty nurse; she justified it by stating she was always forced to be suffocated by her adult clothing. Jules was pretty, slim, and tall but simple, however, like Kat. She was never the center of attention, although she was bold with her work. She was in charge, referred to as the HBIC by her associates. She pulled all the strings and called all the shots. In that way, she was intimidating. She had mousy brown hair and petite features. She was also small-chested, but she warned Kat she would be wearing her most impressive push-up bra that night. Jules had a friend with benefits, as she called him. She typically worked long hours and declared that it was too hard to manage a real relationship. Kat supposed Jules was just scared of change and of commitment. Jules informed Kat that since Baron was joining, she would invite her friend along too.

Kat rummaged through her closet. She was not the dress-up type of girl. She had nearly nothing to delve through. She decided on a pair of black cat ears and some black eyeliner, with whiskers to add. *So spicy, Kat.* She rolled her eyes at herself as she stared at herself in the mirror. *It will have to do.*

Her phone vibrated. Baron had texted, "Should I come up?" Kat wrote back, "No, I am coming down."

As she opened the door, Baron stood there, tall and sexy. He was wearing a cape and vampire teeth with a small amount of blood running from one side. "I want to suck your blood!" he screamed as he picked her up and gnawed at her neck. She laughed and fought her way back to the ground.

"What happened to my hot date?" She giggled as she meddled with his cape. Kat felt like a teenager going on her first date. She had butterflies in her stomach, and she blushed as he kissed her cheek. "Let's go! Off to the club we go!" Kat exclaimed excitedly.

The club was packed with people in costumes. Kat considered herself underdressed for the occasion, but it didn't bother her. She had a hot Latino vampire by her side. He grabbed her hand and escorted her to Jules's table. Introductions were made. Jules's friend had not yet arrived. He was evidently a hippie who had no concept of time, in Jules's words. He was clearly the opposite of her, which possibly was the reason for her attraction and her excuse for not committing. She was usually punctual and tasteful, minus the slutty nurse getup that evening.

Baron and Jules hit it off. They discussed work mainly and some additional activities and such they enjoyed. Scottie, the friend with benefits, arrived nearly an hour late, but that didn't seem to bother Jules. She was dancing and singing along to the music. It was nice to see Jules relax. Kat joined her on the dance floor, leaving Baron to entertain Scottie.

Eventually, Kat's feet needed a break. "I'm taking five, Jules. Need a refreshment!" she shouted as she left the dance floor and returned to the table to join Baron.

"Thanks for being such a good sport," Kat whispered in Baron's ear.

"I think I'm too old for this. My ears are ringing from the loud music," he teased.

"I invited Cindy from the office too!" Jules hollered as she returned to the table. "You may have met her. I can't remember if you were still there or not." She was pointing behind Kat, signaling that Cindy was approaching.

"I don't think so. It doesn't sound familiar," Kat replied.

Just as Kat turned around to greet Cindy, she spotted Amy following closely behind.

"Oh God!" Jules screamed. Jules hustled around the table, placing herself between Kat and Amy.

Kat watched as Jules said something into Cindy's ear. As she did, Amy stepped around her, face-to-face with Jules. Jules and Amy exchanged words as Cindy appeared uncomfortable. They were about four feet away from the table.

Baron slid a hand around one side of Kat's waist. "Is everything OK?" he asked.

"No. I can explain later. Let's get out of here," she said. She clutched Baron's hand and darted toward the door, purposely taking the long route to the exit to avoid Amy. As she left, she turned around to see Amy pointing and shouting something toward Kat. Thankfully, the music was too loud for her to draw attention.

They made it outside the club. "Katherine, you look pale. What was that?" Baron asked.

"That was crazy Amy in the flesh."

"I knew it. I thought it was. I met her once, when you three were having dinner."

"Yeah, I am so sorry. It seems I will never escape this nightmare, and I'm just dragging you along."

"That? That was nothing. We have been through worse." He smirked as he pulled her closer as they walked toward the subway station.

"Again, a great sport you are. I have to be the luckiest unluckiest girl alive, huh?"

They shared another laugh as they jumped onto the subway. "My place?" Baron asked.

"Absolutely," Kat said.

THIRTY-TWO

Several days felt like several weeks. Kat now had her own toothbrush at Baron's. They always stayed at his place. She felt awkward about asking Baron to stay in the home she and Ryan had created—the table they'd picked out together, the bed they'd shared, the shower Ryan had used each morning and night. She knew Baron had concluded that Ryan had killed Sophia; there were no other possibilities in his mind. Although he never mentioned it, she knew. In spite of it all, they were entirely relaxed around each other. They took turns cooking and would argue about who was the better cook. It was obviously Kat.

"Morning, Libby," Kat said as she strolled in. Kat knew no one suspected them at the office. They made sure to keep their interactions professional at work. They rarely had lunch together or even at the same time. Kat sat at the opposite end of the table in meetings, but she would catch Baron watching her from across the table. Kat wasn't embarrassed by the relationship, but neither was ready to be bothered with the questions that would have arisen. Could anyone understand? Everyone speculated that Katherine Letty's dead husband had murdered Baron's niece. Given the awkwardness of that circumstance, they decided together to publicize the relationship at a later time.

Libby wandered in with a coffee cup in hand. She set in on Kat's desk and plopped down in the chair facing Kat. Libby blabbed on and on about her weekend and her dog, Benji. Kat halfheartedly listened and threw in the occasional "Really" to suggest she was indeed listening. Libby was in an extra talkative mood that day, Kat thought. Libby also informed her she had baked cookies and would bring her one later. Finally, the ring of Kat's cell phone saved her.

"I'm sorry, Libby, but I must take this," Kat said.

On the other end of the phone was Detective Ferguson. Another dreaded conversation awaited, she supposed.

Kat hung up the phone with disgust. Her fear had been confirmed. Detective Ferguson had informed Kat that they had closed Sophia's case. Kat believed they would now never know who really had killed her. They had all willed Ryan as a murderer long before closing the case, Kat realized. She'd suspected this eventually would take place. The words were agonizing to hear, although they did not change Kat's thoughts. She understood the closing of the case would, in some sense, bring closure to Baron and his family. Baron had yet to share with his sister and the rest of the family the status of Kat's and his relationship. It was hard even for the two of them to understand, much less outsiders. She often wondered how his family would react—to her especially. Would they welcome her with open arms or resent her for once loving someone they believed had taken away their Sophia? Kat wanted to grieve; she wanted to fall into Baron's arms for consoling. How could she? He would be ecstatic. Justice was served, in his eyes; the healing could now commence for his family.

She called Jules. Jules had a hard time understanding Kat and Baron's connection and their claiming to love each other in something so messy. To her, it seemed too complicated. Kat had already been through so much, and she couldn't fathom why Kat would intentionally subject herself to something else so slippery. She often talked about a clean start, and Kat assumed she meant without Baron. Jules would email her job listings in nearby towns.

Although Kat was appreciative of Jules's support, she was done letting anyone else run her life. For so long, Kat had felt like a fixed object in a room, something that just sat there in its place, like a delicate vase a housekeeper would polish here and there and put right back. She always felt invisible, as if she were playing a part. It hadn't always been like that. At one time, before Noah had died, she had been genuinely happy. Life had been different then—easy. Ryan had been different, and so had Kat. The tragedy of losing Noah had blown up their life and uprooted everything. Kat didn't blame Noah; she blamed herself. Maybe Dr. Phelps was right; another shot at therapy might help.

"How's your day?" Baron asked as he shuffled into her office.

She could tell he had received the same phone call she had. His posture gave it away. He looked almost remorseful, as if he were trying to hide the contentment he felt from the same call that had struck Kat's heart like a knife. Her ache didn't bring him pleasure. He was torn, she knew, between her pain and his relief. Kat didn't say anything. She sat at her desk, looking up at him, searching for a reasonable response.

"Katherine, I am going home for a week. To be with my sister and her family. Tomorrow. Will you be OK?" he asked.

She wasn't OK, but she knew she would be. Space was what they both needed right now. She could try to come to terms with the situation, and so could he. It wasn't feasible for either of them to expect security from another in this situation.

"Yes, absolutely. Your family needs you. I understand," she responded. And she did understand. None of this was his fault; he was dealing with suffering, just as she was.

Baron came around the desk, bent over, placed a hand on hers, and kissed her forehead gently. "I'm sorry, Katherine." He then made his way back around to the door. Before leaving, he turned around. "I will see you tonight. I'm making tacos." He winked at her and left the office.

CHAPTER

THIRTY-THREE

The tacos were fantastic, Kat thought. Baron had Spanish music playing in the kitchen that evening, claiming it added to the authenticity of the tacos he had prepared for her. They never discussed the earlier phone call; both were smart enough to realize nothing positive could come from expanding that conversation. Baron had already packed a suitcase; Kat had noticed it sitting by the front door.

"Your flight is early?" she asked.

"Very. I want to get there early to help organize the ceremony. My family is holding a candlelight vigil, and I thought I should be there to help set up for it," he said.

Sophia was getting a candlelight vigil, and Ryan would have his face blasted all over the papers tomorrow, she expected. Kat felt a hint of resentment in that moment. She excused herself to the restroom to regain her composure. *What if Baron is right? What if Ryan did kill her?* Kat was confused; she didn't want to think about that right now. She poised herself and decided to rejoin Baron and hold him before he left.

Kat never knew Baron left the next morning; he was careful not to wake her. He left a note taped on the mirror: "I love you. I will miss you. See you soon."

On the way to work, Kat received a text from Tom: "Did you see the paper yet?" She had not. She made sure she walked on the opposite side of the newspaper stand so as not to catch a glimpse of the papers. She had heard office chatter of an article being released that day. Someone was always pursuing and printing the latest hot story; she was well aware of the game. She was sure someone had leaked the news of Ryan's guilt intentionally—someone always did. She had her own knowledgeable sources. It was all part of the sport.

She returned a text: "I didn't. I don't want to read it."

Her phone began going off. The remainder of the day brought many texts and calls from random people who had known Ryan. They sent words of encouragement and disbelief. Kat kicked around the idea of holding a memorial for Ryan but decided against it. How could she? After all, he'd been labeled as guilty.

Work was uncomfortable, and even Libby was quiet. Kat concluded that no one knew what to say to her. They pitied her; their expressions told her so. Her coworkers tiptoed around her all day. *It is what it is*, she told herself. Tom invited her to dinner that evening, but Kat politely declined. She wanted a bath and her bed, and that was it. As she grabbed her coat and her bag to leave, her phone rang once more. She let it go to voice mail. She had done enough that day, she decided.

Once home, she warmed up some leftovers from the week that Baron had sent her home with. She had a plate of pasta and a glass of wine. She drew a bath and soaked for more than an hour. She lay in bed and began to filter through the rest of the voice mails. One was from Dr. Phelps's office, reporting that they had her lab results and that she should return the call at her earliest convenience. She was taking the over-the-counter medication recommended and was feeling better.

Kat took a melatonin. She intended to get some rest. The day had exhausted her, but her brain felt busy still. She wanted to call Baron before going to sleep but knew he was at the vigil with his family, so she decided not to distract him.

❧

After making it to work the next morning, Kat began to return phone calls. She refused to disappear again. People had cared about and respected Ryan—at least some had. Kat believed the respectful thing to do was to acknowledge they had reached out to her. She managed to speak with several friends of Ryan in between work emails and calls. The outpouring of sympathy and kindness reassured Kat that Ryan could never have done what he was suspected of. She would not let her love for Baron cloud her judgment.

Baron called Kat that afternoon. He detailed the celebration in Sophia's honor, which Kat found obnoxious. She was certain the ritual had been elaborate; Kat knew a little about Spanish culture from previous work projects and knew Spaniards tended to mourn for long periods of time. She didn't have any feelings about that, but she was feeling slightly defensive that day. Although it was nice to hear his voice, he sounded sincerely cheerful, and for that, she felt bitterness.

"I have to go, Baron; the doctor's office is calling again. I meant to return their call earlier, and I haven't gotten around to it. Talk later. Love you," she said, and she hung up the phone.

"Hello?" Kat said as she answered the call from the doctor's office.

The nurse said hello and went on to explain that all of Kat's labs were normal, with the exception of one: Kat was pregnant.

The nurse was unable to give her details and suggested she make an appointment with an obstetrician.

Kat dropped the phone. *Pregnant? I am pregnant?* The phone screen shattered, but Kat did not move. She was motionless, caught off guard. *I'm pregnant.* A bout of nausea hit her, and she fell to the ground, hurtling herself to the trash can. She immediately scrambled over to her phone and called Jules, still clutching the trash can with her other hand. Thankfully, shattered screen and all, the phone still worked.

Jules met her at her house. Kat had managed to push upstairs to bed. She pulled the covers over her head and began to cry.

Jules joined her on the side of the bed. She lifted up the covers. "Kat, you're going to be fine."

"I don't even know whose baby this is, Jules!" she screamed as she continued to sob. "What if it's Ryan's? What if it's Baron's? We have never discussed having children, and we have been very careful. Oh my God, I am having a branded murderer's baby!" Kat was inconsolable.

Jules let her sob and held her hand.

THIRTY-FOUR

Jules stayed the night with Kat that night. They stayed up half the night, deliberating life and Kat's future. Jules forbade Kat to disappear; she encouraged her to face the situation and jump in headfirst. Kat agreed but was unable to shake a vague feeling that despair could be around the corner. How would Baron react? He was, after all, in his fifties and had grown children. Would he be repulsed by the thought of raising another and perhaps not his own? Kat had not had the opportunity to really think about how she was feeling. She waited for Jules to leave that morning, eagerly wanting to internalize what had transpired the day before. She had found out she was expecting another child. Part of her was elated, and part of her was terrified. She felt impelled into another messy situation. Was their love story doomed? Cursed? Kat questioned it.

Kat decided she would tell Baron when he returned home. There was no need to consume him with the news while he was away, only to leave him to ruminate on it and potentially ruin the rest of the trip. Kat couldn't miss another day of work. Mr. Merrill had been so graciously tolerant and understanding with the Ryan incident that she decided to put her big-girl pants on and head to the office.

She could not help but overanalyze the mistakes she had made with Noah. Had she drunk too much caffeine? Had she eaten too much processed food? Could she have prevented his death? The doctors had reassured Kat many times in the hospital that she was not at fault for his loss of life; however, this pregnancy brought back many emotions and doubts in Kat's mind. She thought about Sophia. *Is this how she felt when she found out she was pregnant—frightened and joyful at the same time?* Kat was now facing the same demise Sophia had faced. Would her lover choose her? *Will he love me and stand beside me in spite of the situation?* With that thought, she felt sorry for Sophia for what she had endured—not only her death but also the events leading up to it, the unknown. This was torture she would not have wished on her worst enemy, not even Sophia.

Enough self-pity, Kat. You've got this, she told herself on her ride to work.

"Morning, Libby," Kat said as she entered.

"Good morning to you, Kat," Libby said.

"Hey!" Kat heard Libby call out. Libby had stood and was now approaching Kat. She gawked down at Kat's feet and began chuckling. Kat looked down to see she had worn one black flat and one brown flat. Both women immediately burst out in laughter.

Kat shrugged and turned away, throwing up her hands. "It's been a rough morning, as you can see." She snickered as she continued moving toward her office. She'd needed a good laugh that morning. *It is what it is,* she thought. *Least of my worries.* Kat was typically dressed proficiently, playing her professional part. She scolded herself. *Do better.*

Work was manageable. Kat had a few meetings scheduled that she crushed, validating her ability of being capable. She could do this. *Day by day,* she thought. Even if Baron decided he couldn't, there were plenty of single mothers out there working and thriving—although she didn't know of any them. That made her laugh out loud. *Wow, Kat, good pep talk with yourself.*

Baron had sent an earlier message to say hello and to let Kat know he was thinking of her. She replied, failing to mention the new life-altering news. "All is well here," she lied.

Kat called her obstetrician, the same one she had seen when she was pregnant with Noah. They scheduled her for an examination in one week. What a shit show of a story she would present to the doctor: "Hey, I'm pregnant and not sure whose baby this is: my accused-murderer husband, who is now deceased, or my current lover, who happens to be the uncle of the murdered."

This is a Lifetime movie, she thought, and her cheeks became flushed at the thought. *How humiliating.* Kat's plan was to see the doctor before unloading the news on Baron. She wanted details, such as how far along she was, to be able to relay some specifics to him.

Jules told Kat she would take the afternoon off to escort her to the doctor. She reassured Kat that everything was fine and stressed that she had obviously made it through the worst. Worst-case scenario, Kat was a single mother who'd lost the love of her life. No big deal.

Kat shrugged as she listened to Jules. *Nice, Jules. Another uplifting pep talk for the day,* she grumbled in her mind. She knew Jules was only making light of it all, and she was sure Jules had faith that Kat could conquer even this. Kat loved that Jules brought some lighthearted humor to the heavy conversation.

Mr. Merrill popped his head in. He delicately informed Kat that the magazine would be writing and featuring a piece on Sophia. He was respectful in his presentation, believing the news would be difficult for Kat to hear. He also informed her she would not have to be part of it; he was only forewarning her.

More great news, she silently said to herself. *Mark this week down, Kat; this was a doozy.* Kat nodded and smiled, careful not to display any hard feelings, assuring him she understood.

That evening, Jules called Kat once again. "You don't have to babysit me, Jules," Kat said before saying hello.

"I'm not. I have some news," Jules said with excitement.

"I hope it's good. If not, save it for tomorrow, please. I'm done with today."

"Amy is moving! She handed her notice in today. Apparently, she got a job in California."

Kat sighed with relief. "OK, that *is* good news. I was due for some good news." The news thrilled Kat; the idea of running into Amy was appalling. They frequented the same grocery stores, restaurants, and coffee shops, so the probability was high. The large city felt tiny at times. Kat was relieved and grateful for the news. She didn't even ask why Amy had decided to relocate; she just soaked in the encouraging update.

THIRTY-FIVE

Baron returned home and appeared unquestionably eager as Kat stood in the kitchen upon his arrival. He wasted no time in invading Kat. He ravished her like a lion with its prey. She was turned on by his aggressive performance and caved in like the Grand Canyon. She wasn't thinking about the dreaded bombshell she was about to drop on him; she was immersed in his hands and the way they handled her body with such aggressiveness and tenderness mixed in one motion. His hands were soft and slow but firm. Although she never had believed her sex life with Ryan was dull, it definitely never had been as mature and satisfying as her sex with Baron.

After the escapade on the kitchen table and then the bedroom, they sat to eat, both wearing smiles. Kat had ordered takeout from Baron's favorite sushi spot. While he devoured a hand roll, Kat stiffened up while she asked him how he would feel about having another child. Just like that, she blitzed him with a million-dollar question.

Baron laughed and looked up at her. "Is this a serious question, Katherine?"

"What if it were?" she said.

"Well, I would consider having that conversation with you,

of course. I would never aspire to deny you of having your own. I am a bit old. Don't you agree? That's a tricky question, I suppose."

He was now perched over his hand roll, emotionless, waiting or Kat's rebuttal. She could see frustration flooding his being. He seemed oddly confused by her expression, as if he were trying to get to the bottom of the banter.

"Katherine, you look as if you have seen a ghost. What's going on?" he asked.

"I'm pregnant, Baron," she said.

He set his roll back on his plate and observed her. "Pregnant?" he asked, baffled. "We have been very cautious. Not to say it's not possible, but are you certain?"

"I am going to the ob-gyn in a few days. I intended on waiting to tell you, but I couldn't. A urine test at my last appointment established it."

He stood up from the table and instantly made his way to Kat to embrace her. "Wow, Katherine, we are having a baby! *Starting over* is an understatement." He beamed as he held her closely. "Are you OK with this? My kids won't believe this. You haven't met my boys; you have to meet my boys."

Kat could tell Baron's mind was racing. He was enthusiastic. She had not expected this reaction. Kat said she wanted to halt any additional discussion with each other or family and did not want to disclose any further facts until after she saw the doctor, and Baron agreed. If her premonition was correct, this was not Baron's baby.

The last few days of the week lingered on. Fortunately for Kat, they were ordinary and uninteresting. She had learned to appreciate the dull days and even welcomed them. Baron continually sent her texts about the baby, as well as healthy diet and other books to read. Kat considered it a tad overboard, but she was smitten with his excitement. It would be short-lived, she feared.

Tom texted again that morning, inviting Kat for dinner. She hated to disappoint him yet again, so she agreed to meet after work. Baron didn't seem to mind; he urged Kat to have a great evening but to be careful and to let him know when she made it home safe and sound. He was more protective than usual, which she found comforting. She would enjoy it while it lasted, she supposed.

Kat decided not to tell Tom she was pregnant. She refused a glass of chardonnay, which Tom found strange and called her out on. She appeased him with an excuse about having to work later on a time-sensitive project, and the lie sufficed. Tom seemed to be doing well. He mentioned Amy was moving.

"Are you two speaking again?" Kat asked.

"Not really. I guess she wanted me to know she was moving is all. She is difficult, Kat. I don't know why we keep doing this on-and-off-again thing."

Difficult was not the word Kat would have used to describe Amy. *She is a lying, manipulative, evil being—that is what she is.* Kat wanted to scream and shake some sense into Tom. *She is using you! You are her backup plan!* But she didn't; she listened as he vented.

They reminisced about Ryan a little, and Tom told some stories Kat had not heard. It was nice to hear Ryan's name. She wondered how Baron would have felt if he knew they were chitchatting about old times with Ryan, the wicked assassin. She felt no shame, only a hint of guilt.

Tom asked her about Sophia. He had read the recent article about the investigation being concluded. "Who killed her, Kat?" he asked.

Amy is my guess, she thought. "I don't know. But I do know Ryan did not. It's a shame. Now we will never know," she replied.

Kat woke the next morning with a dry mouth. She was anxious about her doctor's appointment that afternoon. She had convinced Baron to let her make the first trip alone. She was terrified he would discover the time frame did not add up and realize the baby was not his. He clearly assumed the baby was his. Did he think she was only a couple of weeks along? She didn't try to figure it out; she rolled with it. Maybe his overexcitement blurred his reality. Who knew? Kat also failed to reveal that Jules was accompanying her, knowing that would break his heart.

Kat wept as the doctor left the room. Jules remained beside her, handing her the box of tissues sitting on the counter. The conception date had been revealed. Kat remembered the exact night. Ryan had taken her to the grand opening of a new restaurant near their home. They had made love twice that evening after returning home. She vividly recalled the details of that night. It had been the first time she witnessed remorse in Ryan's face.

Kat was much further along than she'd anticipated. She had not started showing at all, and the doctor convinced her that was normal and that the baby looked healthy. She refused the announcement of the sex of the baby. She wanted it to be a surprise, something to look forward to in her future.

THIRTY-SIX

Jules didn't offer advice on when and how to tell Baron. She knew Kat was determined about becoming more independent with her decisions. She would be there to help her pick up the pieces if Baron decided to jump ship.

Kat internally deliberated waiting to tell him and holding on to him as long as she could. She knew she could choose not to tell him at all, and she considered that. She told Jules, and Jules did offer a comment there, one of her well-known lighthearted, sarcastic remarks: "Kat, he's tall and dark, not to mention he's a Spanish man—the opposite of Ryan. Pretty certain this baby will be distinctly pure Caucasian, not to mention Baron can add." Pouting dramatically, Kat knew she could never be capable of that sort of disloyalty.

Kat intentionally avoided Baron at the office. He sent a few texts asking about the appointment, asking for details. She answered vaguely and told him they could talk about it later. He agreed. He had two client meetings scheduled for the day, and she knew they would entertain the majority of his day. Kat normally would have pouted about such and sought out his attention, but that day was different.

Baron and Kat made plans to meet at Lindens for appetizers

and a celebratory nonalcoholic drink after work. He used the word *celebratory*, not Kat. She managed to dodge him all day, minus the small mishap down the hall when he slapped her butt unsuspiciously as she passed by to the copy room. She decided that if he were to call it quits, she would undoubtedly have to find a new job. She would not be able to face him each day, and she was certain he would feel the same. She was already jumping to conclusions.

Lindens was packed. Baron texted Kat and told her to take her time, as they had a forty-five-minute wait for a table. Kat went home after work to check her mail, tidy up, and change. She wanted to look suitable and attractive, as she potentially would be begging for reconsideration that night and wanted to look good for it. She realized she was not nearly as confident in the relationship as she had believed she was. This was major: choosing to raise another man's child, a man he despised.

Kat arrived; Baron was sitting at the table with sparkling water waiting for her. He stood to pull out her chair and kissed her lips before returning to his seat.

"Would you mind if I ordered a bourbon?" he asked.

"Of course not." She laughed. "You aren't pregnant."

Kat lost her nerve at the restaurant. As they wandered home, she persuaded herself that telling him in private would be the decent thing to do. She recognized she was just afraid, scared of his reaction. She again succeeded in derailing each question about her due date and such with vague responses. She told him the ob-gyn had done blood tests, and she would have a sonogram next time, which was a lie. She told him the doctor had assured her that the heartbeat sounded strong and that she didn't see any concerns with Kat's blood pressure. *Pull the damn Band-Aid off, Kat,* she told herself as they strolled the streets back to her place.

When they arrived back at Kat's house, they stopped before entering. Baron still had not stepped foot inside, so she knew this meant they would say goodbye at her doorstep.

"Baron, would you like to come up?" she asked apprehensively.

He stuttered, "Come up inside? I am not confident I am ready for that." He looked down at the ground. He was like a kid kicking a rock, moving his foot back and forth on a playground, waiting to be picked for wall ball.

"This is my house; these are my things, not just his. I took pictures of us down, Baron. I mean, it's part of who I am too, you know," she said softly.

He nodded as she grabbed his hand and squeezed. She led him inside and shut the door. They went into the living area. She caught him looking around, searching for evidence of Ryan's presence. She sat first and patted the couch. "Sit down by me," she said.

He obliged. She could tell he was uncomfortable. He was silent, and his face had reddened. His body was tense, and his hand shook as she held it.

"Baron, we need to talk," she said.

"I'm sorry. I'm trying, Katherine. I am. This is hard for me. I believe in my soul that he killed her. If I didn't love you so much, I would run—race right out of here. It makes me angry. Please understand I am still angry."

"I do understand. It was a bad idea to ask you to come in. It's just—" She went silent.

"It's just what?" he asked. He stood up and began to pace the room, looking around impatiently. "I don't feel comfortable here," he said.

"Please sit back down. I have to tell you something," she said.

The veins had begun to bulge from his head and neck, and his jaw was clenched. Kat began to cry, crumbling over the slightest bit of pressure, just like she used to. Baron headed toward the door and yanked it open; he stood there watching her cry. Kat sprang forward toward him and attempted to grab his hands. He was rigid and visibly shaken.

"Can we please just step outside, Katherine?" he asked strongly.

"Yes, yes," she said as she followed him out. She managed to dry her tears with her jacket.

"I'm not trying to upset you; I don't like to see you cry. It's just that I wasn't ready for that. I wasn't. I should have known better. I can usually contain myself—the anger. But I wasn't able to, and I apologize."

"Baron, the baby isn't yours," she said. The courage came from nowhere. The words rolled out of her mouth like a red carpet for a great musician.

He glared at her. "What!" he shouted. "What are you saying, Katherine? What do you mean the baby isn't mine?" he asked, this time slightly calmer.

"It's Ryan's. I must have—" She didn't get to finish her sentence before he began pacing and hollering, throwing his hands around in the air.

"How could you? I can't believe you would keep this from me. What the hell, Katherine? Why have you led me to believe it was mine? Is there something wrong with you?" he screamed as he stepped away farther and farther from her.

The shock of the revelation was overpowering, and he began moving erratically all over the sidewalk. Kat's head began to throb, and she felt weak. She had never seen him like this, and she was concerned by it. "Please calm down." She raised her voice at him.

He gathered some composure. "I have to collect myself. I must go," he calmly said before turning to walk away.

Kat stood there on the sidewalk alone, watching as he walked away. He made it to the corner before hailing a cab and disappearing into the crowded streets.

THIRTY-SEVEN

Kat did not attempt to contact Baron. She did him a favor by resigning immediately from the *Daily*. Kat knew he could never love her child the way it deserved to be loved. The child was innocent, just as Kat felt she was. She chose not to fight for Baron, but she wasn't rolling over either. She fully intended on providing an appropriate life for her baby. She was hopeful that someday she would get what she deserved, even if it didn't include a knight in shining armor. But she had love. She already loved this child the way she loved Noah. She didn't blame Baron for her heartache; she couldn't love him properly either. She read in a magazine a small piece that struck a chord: "Whether this love story unfolds gracefully or falls apart in pieces, it will still be a story I will always remember." The line summed up exactly how Kat felt. She had come to terms with the fact that not every love story ended in happily ever after. There was something to be said about the beginning and the middle of the story. It was still love.

It took her two weeks to determine where she would depart to—where she would begin again. She took Jules's advice and decided to restart, recharge, and revive in another town in another state. Katherine Letty, plus one, was moving to

Connecticut. She would still have access to the big city to visit Jules and to finalize the selling of her home. Connecticut school systems were categorized as some of the best in the country; she would get to experience every single season of the year; and from what she heard, fall was breathtaking there.

After deciding on her new homestead and speaking with the Realtor about selling her home, she decided to gather all the documents regarding the home. Every legal file she and Ryan had ever had was stored in the safe. She had locked it up after the officers rummaged throughout the house, never to reopen it. When they'd purchased the house, they had been given a plan and miniature layout with every detail, even light sockets. Kat had found it helpful when purchasing lamps and furniture and preferred to pass it along to the new owners.

As Kat fumbled through the paperwork, she came across a handwritten letter dated the day of Ryan's death. The police had missed it, as it had been meticulously placed in between several of the pieces of paper and stapled along with them carefully.

> Dear Kat,
> If you are reading this, then I know you have moved on and are selling our home. I know you all too well. I knew you would want to share these specifics with the new owners. You were always so considerate of others, putting everyone ahead of yourself. I remember you that way. I painstakingly write this letter, as these will be the last words you will ever hear from me. I have loved three people in my life: my mother, you, and Noah. I am sorry for the decisions I made and was petrified that someday you would forgive me and come home. I am no good. I

don't deserve you. I could never let that happen, so I am taking my life. I lied to you, Kat. I did kill her. I turned into someone even I did not recognize. I am deeply sorry to leave you with the burden of wearing my name; it's tarnished. I hope that someday you find the happiness you deserve—the happiness you had the day in the park when you told me you were pregnant. I lost myself somewhere in the middle of all this. Do with this letter what you would like. I am ashamed of what I have done to you and to her. Without you, I feel like a lost soul aimlessly wandering this earth. I am not blaming you. We all heal in different ways. I never healed. I never recovered, and for that, I am sorry. I was not the strong man I professed to be. I asked you to forgive me, but I didn't mean it. I was only scared—scared of the realization of who I really was, who I had become. I am taking the easy way out. One final disappointment. I do not write this letter for sympathy, only to sincerely apologize and to tell you the truth. I love you, Kat, always and forever.

Love,

Ryan

Kat's hands trembled, and she felt as if she might explode or faint at any time. She could barely read the last few lines through her tears. He had killed Sophia. She had been wrong all along. The tension tugged at her temples. She felt fury surging through her veins. She hit the ground so hard it pained her knuckles. After everything, now she'd found this letter, an admission of guilt left for her. She screamed out loud, "You coward! How dare you!"

She lay in bed, clenching the letter, recollecting all the times she had defended him and his character. She was embarrassed—humiliated at herself. How had she not seen it? Why had she always been so reluctant to hear the evidence? She never had sat down with Ferguson and had that conversation. She had been in denial. Maybe she just hadn't wanted to believe she could be that naive and foolish. Kat folded the letter up and put it back in the safe.

CHAPTER
THIRTY-EIGHT

Moving day arrived. Jules showed up to help direct the movers. Mainly, she had control issues and wanted to be sure everything was packed and stacked appropriately. Kat let Jules oversee the packing and stacking. The moving van and crew were a going-away gift from Jules. Kat was appreciative, but she would have hired them anyway. Jules was afraid Kat would try to do too much, and she considered her fragile. "I'm just pregnant, Jules, not breakable," Kat argued.

Kat had purchased a little farmhouse with one acre in Columbia, Connecticut. It was about a three-hour drive from Manhattan. With a population of five thousand, Columbia was small-town living with many popular attractions. It was known for repeat summer vacations to Columbia Lake and hiking trails. Kat was eager for a different existence; she was excited about this new chapter. She was hesitant in sharing the actual story of Katherine Benson, so instead, she called herself a pregnant widow who had lost her husband in a tragic car accident. She started a new job as a library assistant at the public library. Kat didn't need the money; she enjoyed the library. It was peaceful, and she felt surrounded by hard work and courage. She admired people brave enough and willing to share their stories or to put their thoughts on paper for the world to evaluate—minus a suicide note. That was spineless.

Her new life felt complete—almost. Kat was patiently anticipating the arrival of her baby. She transferred her care to the town obstetrician and developed a bond with her. They even became friends, having lunch occasionally and discussing life and pregnancy. She was due in less than two weeks, and Jules planned to stay with Kat for a few days during and after the birth. Jules visited frequently, remaining devoted and helpful. Jules would drive up and spend a weekend here and there, referring to it as camping, although it was a farmhouse, not a cabin, and it was nothing like camping. Jules decided Kat had fallen in love with herself again, complimenting her frequently. Jules was proud of her; plus, she secretly enjoyed the country life, although she never admitted it. Kat missed the city sometimes; her jogs through the city had been her savior countless times. She would forever be grateful to the city for that.

Jules helped Kat prepare the baby's room. Kat selected a pale yellow accent wall, with a cream rocking chair exactly like the one she'd had for Noah. Kat had moments when she longed for Baron. She missed him. Just as she had with the old rocker, she would sit and cry, finding comfort in the chair. She thought of what could have been. It had been nearly six months; she was sure he had moved on by now. He never once reached out, which frustrated her sometimes. She knew realistically that was easiest for him and for her. *Why didn't he fight for me?* Maybe he had fooled her, just as Ryan had.

A surprise email that morning perked Kat up. It was from Libby—just a hello with some additional office drama. Libby noted that she disliked Kat's replacement and that she missed her and thought of her often. In further chatting, Kat discovered that Baron had resigned a few months after Kat had. Kat wanted to ask where he had gone but wasn't sure she wanted to know. Had he met someone and whisked her away? Were they out traveling the world, as he and Kat had joked about doing so many times, running away with each other? *Kat, break out of it.* To the library she headed.

Kat socialized with all the library regulars. Work was something she looked forward to. She had met some salt-of-the-earth people, and she was excited about raising her baby in a small town. The ladies at the library even had thrown Kat a baby shower. She knew someone just about everywhere she went at this point. It was comforting. Some would even rub her belly as if they had known Kat all her life.

Kat was cleaning up behind the counter, when Mrs. Berry emerged. "Kat, would you mind putting up this stack of books for me, dear? And use the cart, honey. I don't want you carrying all those books. Might just throw you into labor right here in the library. Now, I've delivered a baby, but it's been a lifetime ago."

Kat laughed. "Yes, Mrs. Berry, I will use the cart."

Mrs. Berry was an older lady in her mideighties. She considered herself the town mayor, but technically, Mr. Berry held that title. The whole town knew who pulled the strings, though.

Kat loaded the books onto the cart, as Mrs. Berry had asked. As Kat rounded the *M*-through-*P* section, she saw him standing there looking straight at her.

"Baron." Kat blinked a few times to be sure he wasn't a pregnancy haze or a figment of her imagination.

THIRTY-NINE

"Hello, Katherine," Baron said. He was more handsome than Kat remembered.

Kat paused; she was speechless. Part of her ached to run to him and throw her arms around him, but she remained still. The other half seized control. She felt dazed, somewhat numb, and a bit angry.

"Katherine Benson, is it?" he asked quietly, almost whispering, while flickering a small grin. "You weren't hard to find. Seems everyone here knows you."

Kat remained silent, confused, waiting for an explanation. He crept a few feet closer, and she could smell his cologne. He didn't appear nervous, although his hands were wedged in his pockets.

"Can we talk?" he asked softly.

Kat ignored the question briefly as she looked around the library. It was fairly empty that day; a few older ladies gathered around a round table about twenty-five feet away. She wondered where Mrs. Berry was, almost as if she would march around the corner to save her or tell her to get back to work, which was ridiculous. Mrs. Berry would probably have given Kat's company a hug and told her to take all the time she needed with her visitor.

Kat had waited for this day to come, and now that it had, she was undecided on how to react. To her surprise, she was cautious and leery. Her heart and her mind were not on the same page evidently.

"How did you find me?" she finally asked timidly. She began anxiously rubbing her belly. They continued to whisper back and forth.

"Any time now, huh? Are you having a girl or a boy?" he asked, unintentionally dodging her question.

"Baron, what are you doing here?" she asked.

He moved toward her, reaching out his arms and leaning in to hug her. She indulged and embraced him back. He felt just as she recalled, strong but warm.

"Katherine, can we talk?" he asked again.

"I'm working," she answered with an indifferent expression on her face.

"I meant later. I'm staying at the bed-and-breakfast on Tate Avenue. Please," he pleaded.

"You're staying here in Columbia?" she said. Baron had stepped back to give her some space. Kat fidgeted with the books on the cart, failing to make eye contact with him.

"Katherine," he said. She loved the way he said her name; it made her weak in the knees.

Katherine agreed to meet Baron that evening. She gave him her address, and then he disappeared as quickly as he had arrived.

Kat immediately called Jules in a panic from the restroom. She began to sob while she explained to Jules how Baron had shown up. Kat then played twenty questions with Jules, who asked, "Why is he there? Does he want you back?" Kat clarified she only had agreed to meet him later and could not answer her questions yet.

Katherine hurried home. She wanted to freshen up and tidy the house before Baron arrived. Kat's judgment was clouded and blurry. Baron always seemed to have that effect on her. The truth was, her heart wanted to snatch him up and play house for the rest of eternity, but her mind told her to remain guarded. After all, he had run away never to return—but he had returned.

She heard the knock.

"Come in." Kat motioned him inside. "Welcome to my home." She greeted him with a modest smile. She hesitated as he reached out to her. "I'm sorry. I just didn't expect to see you again," she said.

The house was warm, with a comfy feel. She had made the place her own. It was nothing fancy but was cozy. She had a large sectional one could get lost in, with blankets spread across the back. Several pillows were stacked against one another. Jules called it a country ambience. Kat had cleaned up before his arrival, and each pillow was in its exact place. On the entrance table, she had lit a candle that smelled of citrus.

Baron looked around as he entered. He stopped and gazed at the picture beside the candle. It was a framed print of her sonogram. He admired it momentarily before looking up.

"You look wonderful, Katherine. You really do," he said.

They briefly chatted about her pregnancy and her new home. Kat proudly offered him a tour of her new home, and he accepted. She was proud of her new place and her new life, overlooking the elephant in the room: his presence.

"I was not prepared to have company, obviously. I would be glad to reheat some soup from last night if you are hungry," she said.

"No, don't go to any trouble. I wanted to sit and talk—talk about the night I left you, Katherine. My emotions got the best of me. I came to genuinely apologize. I never should have walked away from you. I left you confused that night, standing there alone on the sidewalk. Not a day goes by that I don't regret it." A single tear rolled down his cheek. His face was red, and he occasionally ran his hands through his hair. Kat recognized that was a nervous habit of his.

As they stood there in the living room, Katherine began to cry. "I am still confused, Baron. I thought you loved me."

"I do love you. I was overjoyed you were pregnant. Then going into his home that night and having you break that news to me stunned me. I felt broken and furious. And the truth is, I didn't know how to react. The anger took over. I did the only thing I could: walk away. I didn't want to say anything I would regret. The irony is that I do regret it. I regret everything about that night," he said.

Baron took a seat on the couch, looking up at Kat with sincerity in his eyes. "There is more, Katherine," he said. "Ferguson and I became friends throughout the investigation and kept in touch regularly. New evidence developed shortly after you left town that pointed to a new suspect. Apparently, Ferguson was never able to let the case go and never trusted that Ryan was guilty. Ferguson proclaimed Ryan was a smart man, and some damning DNA evidence evolved after they found Sophia's body. DNA labs were shorthanded, so evidence was taking longer to process, and just as Ferguson thought, new DNA evidence confirmed Ryan was innocent. The papers didn't publicize the findings, knowing the NYPD would catch flak, so they kept it quiet. He eventually shared this news with me, convincing me of Ryan's innocence. The case was reopened, Katherine, and they have made an arrest."

Kat took a seat beside him, baffled. She remained silent.

"They arrested Amy Harris. Her DNA was found

underneath Sophia's fingernails. There were threatening text messages to Sophia the night she disappeared, all from Amy. You were right, Katherine. I am sorry."

Kat sat back on the couch, shocked. She knew that was not accurate. Ryan had confessed to her in his letter. Amy must have visited Sophia that evening before Ryan did, Kat thought, and an altercation had occurred between the two women—that was the only logical explanation.

"I should have heard you out, Katherine. I never should have walked away from you. I should have understood you were also grieving a loss. I was selfish. I was stubborn," he said.

Still, Kat was taken aback by the news. She struggled with how to respond to Baron. After all, she knew Amy was innocent. She knew Ryan had murdered Sophia in cold blood.

Despite all the turmoil and confusion, Kat was certain of one thing: she was still in love with Baron. Seeing him again face-to-face had reignited the spark of her blazing desire for him.

She had a choice: she could do the right thing and confess to Baron her knowledge of Amy's innocence or remain silent and let an innocent woman who'd betrayed her take the fall.

"Katherine, are you OK?" he asked as grasped her hand and held it up. "You're bleeding."

Kat had anxiously and unknowingly chewed her nail down to the cuticle, and it was now bleeding. "Oh goodness," she said as she stood and headed toward the kitchen. She turned on the faucet and ran water over her hand.

Baron followed. He asked again, "Are you OK?"

Kat was somewhat staggered, continuing to process the news about Amy. "Yeah, yeah, I'm fine," she said as she turned off the faucet and grabbed a paper towel to wrap around her finger.

Baron moved closer to Kat in the kitchen. He unwrapped

her finger from the paper towel and examined it. "I think it stopped bleeding; I think you're going to make it," he teased as he flashed her a slight grin while rewrapping it. "But I should probably hang around just to make sure it heals up, OK?" He laughed.

"I'd like that," she responded as she placed her head on his chest.

Baron wrapped his arms around Kat, squeezing her tightly. "I have missed you," he whispered.

That instant, she made her choice. She chose happiness. She chose herself and a future with Baron.

As they left the kitchen, she let out a sigh of relief. She felt secure in her decision. Baron followed her back to the sofa, and they sat.

"Kat, I'm staying in Columbia for a few days. Or possibly longer," he said as he shrugged and silently pleaded with his eyes. He waited for a response, appearing eager for an answer or an invitation. "I retired from the *Daily*, you know," he said as he ran his fingers through his hair. She knew he was nervously awaiting her reply.

Kat nodded as she looked down at the paper towel around her finger.

"I have been staying in New Jersey with my son," he added.

Kat looked up at him. "Columbia is a beautiful town," she replied as she smiled at him. "But it has been a big day, Baron. Can we call it a night? I'm tired, and this is a lot to process."

"Of course," he replied as he stood up from the couch.

Kat walked Baron to the door. "I'm glad you're here. I really am."

He gave her one last hug before walking out.

After Baron left that night, Kat built a fire in her fire pit out back. It was May, obviously too hot for a fire, but Kat had plans. She dug through a shoebox hidden underneath her bed and found Ryan's letter.

Baron called Kat before bed. After two hours on the phone, she heard a tap on the door. "I have to go, Baron; someone is at my door. Talk tomorrow." She hung up the phone and answered the door.

To her surprise, Baron was standing on the doorstep, holding his suitcase. "I will spend the rest of my life right here on this doorstep if you don't let me in. I will never walk away from you and our baby again. The world is cold and lonely without you, and I want this. I want you."

☙❧

The labor went as anticipated, and the nurses laid a healthy baby girl in Kat's arms as she cried, this time happy tears. Baron and Jules remained bedside, elated.

Kat sat up, holding the most beautiful baby girl she had ever seen. As she handed her to Baron, she whispered, "Meet our baby girl, Sophia."

Made in the USA
Columbia, SC
05 August 2023

21273896R00138